"Hey, Heather!" Joe called out, and he headed over to her. He followed her onto the baseball field, allowing himself to imagine what it would be like to be in the stadium not as a fan, but as a baseball star, one who would impress a certain attractive photographer.

Joe glanced at Heather but did a double take when he saw the sudden change in her expression. Her smile disappeared, and her brown eyes opened wide with fear.

"Joe!" she shouted. "Look out!"

Joe spun around too late.

Three baseballs were rocketing straight for his head!

Books in THE HARDY BOYS CASEFILES® Series

Available from ARCHWAY Paperbacks

THE HARDY BOYS NO. 46
CASEFILES

FOUL PLAY

FRANKLIN W. DIXON

AN ARCHWAY PAPERBACK
Published by POCKET BOOKS
New York   London   Toronto   Sydney   Tokyo   Singapore

AN ARCHWAY PAPERBACK *Original*

An Archway Paperback published by
POCKET BOOKS, a division of Simon & Schuster Inc.
1230 Avenue of the Americas, New York, NY 10020

ISBN: 0-671-70043-X

First Archway Paperback printing December 1990

10 9 8 7 6 5 4 3 2 1

Printed in the U.S.A.

IL 7+

Chapter

1

"WHAT'S HAPPENING, BRO?" Joe Hardy called out as he stomped through the front door. The athletic, muscular seventeen-year-old spiraled a battered old leather football into the air and then caught it.

Joe's blond hair was messy, his face was bright red, and his blue eyes sparkled—all the result of a game of football played in the near-freezing weather Bayport was experiencing.

"Hey," Frank grunted. Joe's brother, older by a year, looked up briefly, then turned his brown eyes back to the catalog in his lap.

"Still don't know what to get Callie for Christmas, huh?" Joe asked, referring to Frank's long-time girlfriend. He tossed the football into the entryway closet, hung up his parka, then went into the den. Pulling a chair in front of the fire, he plopped down and turned his palms to the flames. A log popped, and small orange sparks flew into the air.

"This is *niiice* and toasty," Joe said. "It's freezing out there."

"Uh-huh," Frank replied flatly. He had stopped turning the pages and stared at the catalog with vacant eyes.

Joe leaned over to get a look at the page at which Frank had stopped.

"I don't think Callie's going to be happy with a table saw," Joe said, grinning. "She would probably like something a little more feminine, don't you think?"

Frank groaned. Closing the catalog, he let the big book drop to the floor. He pulled a lever on the side of his chair and leaned back, propping his feet on top of the footrest as it slid up into place.

"I can't believe I waited until just a week before Christmas to start looking for a gift," Frank said, running a hand through his dark hair.

Joe couldn't resist the opportunity to tease his brother. "It's like I was telling Chet: You let a girl wrap you around her finger, and you'll end up looking like a human pretzel." Joe laughed.

When Frank didn't answer and just kept staring straight at the fire, Joe went on. "Wow. I can't even get you mad at me. Are you feeling all right?"

Frank ignored Joe's dig. "By the way, where is Chet?" he asked in reference to Chet Morton, the Hardys' best friend.

"He had to go home," said Joe. "Where's Dad?"

"In his office packing up some stuff to take with him to New York," Frank replied.

Frank and Joe's mother, Laura Hardy, and their aunt Gertrude were in New York City visiting relatives until Saturday, two days before Christmas. Fenton was leaving later in the evening to join them.

"Well," said Joe, reaching over and throwing another log on the fire, "you can sit around here feeling sorry for yourself, but I'm going to fix myself a sandwich."

As Joe stood the doorbell rang, the chimes pelting out a tinny version of "Jingle Bells." The sound made his teeth tingle, and he shuddered as the last note faded.

He grimaced and turned to Frank. "I wish Mom hadn't talked you into installing that dumb song," he mumbled over his shoulder as he went to answer the door.

Joe opened the door and saw a short man standing on the stoop, stamping his feet in the cold. Pale blue eyes stared at Joe from the man's round, fleshy face. He was wearing orange ear-muffs and a gray wool coat and slacks. A clip-board was tucked under one arm. Joe's eyes landed on a neatly stitched patch over the man's left pocket that read "Bayport Courier Service."

"May I help you?" Joe asked, his breath mak-ing small, cloudlike puffs in the freezing air as the words left his mouth. He shivered from the cold.

The courier coughed, then cleared his throat. "I have a delivery here for a"—he looked at his clipboard—"for an F. Hardy," he announced in a gravelly voice.

"I'm Joe Hardy. I'll take it." Joe reached out his hand.

"Sorry, pal," the courier replied. "This deliv-ery is insured. I gotta have F. Hardy himself sign for it. Nobody else."

"I'm Frank Hardy."

Joe turned as his brother joined him at the door.

The courier's pale eyes focused on Frank. "Got any ID?"

Frank pulled his wallet from his back pocket and flipped it open, revealing his driver's license in the plastic sleeve.

"Okay." The courier held up the clipboard and handed Frank a pen. "I need your signature here." He pointed with his free hand.

After Frank signed his name, the courier un-

4

zipped his jacket, pulled out a small brown envelope, and handed it to Frank.

"Happy holidays," the man said in his gravelly voice. Then he turned and left.

Joe shut the door and followed Frank back into the den. "What's in the envelope?"

"That's what I'm about to find out," Frank replied. Sitting back down in the lounge chair, he turned the envelope over in his hands and saw the Bayport Courier Service label on the front. Whatever was in it was flat and square and smaller than a postcard.

"Who's it from?" Joe asked.

Frank checked the label. "It doesn't say."

"That's odd," Joe said. "Especially since it was insured."

"Hmmm." Frank carefully pulled at the taped end of the envelope and unfolded it.

"Well?" Joe's voice rose, his curiosity getting the better of him.

"Calm down, I'm getting to it." Shooting his brother a mischievous glance, Frank pulled the contents of the envelope out so that it was shielded from Joe's inquisitive eyes.

"So?" Joe said impatiently.

"A baseball card."

"Come on. Stop kidding me." Joe leaned forward to take a closer look.

"Would I ever lie to you?" Frank joked.

Sure enough, inside a plastic sleeve was a

baseball card, an old one. The photo was of a plump young baseball player in an old-fashioned uniform with puffed-out, knicker-length pants. The player's smile was genuine, but his rosy cheeks were an unnatural addition by an artist. At the bottom of the card the player's name was printed: "Honus Wagner."

"Wow!" Joe shouted. "Do you know what you have here?" His face lit up, and his blue eyes shone. "Honus Wagner cards are just about impossible to find."

Frank glanced at the card again. "It's not from you?"

"Me?" Joe looked at Frank as if he were crazy.

"Yeah. You know, an early Christmas gift."

"No way. I got you the same thing I got you last year: a pair of socks."

"Who would send me a rare old baseball card? I haven't collected baseball cards since junior high school."

"Callie?" Joe suggested.

"No," Frank replied. "She already gave me her present. It's under the tree, still wrapped."

"Well, all I can say is, if this is real, you're one rich guy!"

"Well, there's one way to find out," said Frank. He rose from the chair and took the card from Joe. "The baseball shop at the mall."

Joe nodded. "Let's go!"

*　　*　　*

Half an hour later, Joe impatiently drummed his fingers on the glass countertop in the baseball novelty shop. His quick gaze flew over the shelves of baseball caps, T-shirts, cards, and pennants that were packed into the crowded little store. More valuable items—such as signed baseballs and shoes, bats, and gloves that had been used by major-league baseball stars of the past and present—were locked in the glass display case and in glass-enclosed shelves that lined the wall behind the counter. About a half dozen browsers were sifting through old uniforms hanging against a side wall.

Joe already felt as if he knew the whole store by heart. Lyle McKay, owner of the Old Ball Park, had been carefully turning the card over and over for ten minutes. Now he was looking closely at the two-by-three-inch card with a jeweler's glass. His thin gray hair had fallen forward over his forehead, and his long, angular face was tense with concentration.

"Well," said Joe impatiently, "is it the real thing or not?"

Frank elbowed his brother in the ribs. Mr. McKay was nearly seventy years old. He had known Frank and Joe for years, especially Frank, who had frequented the baseball novelty shop when he was younger. Frank didn't want to hurry the man.

"Yep," McKay said in a slow drawl. "Yessirree.'' He raised his eyebrow, and the jeweler's glass popped out and dropped into his waiting hand. Then he gave the card back to Frank.

"I'd put that in a safe place if I were you, Frank," McKay told him a low whisper.

"How come?" Frank asked. He didn't know why, but he was whispering, too.

The gray-haired man leaned forward, signaling for Frank and Joe to do the same. Then, very softly, he said, "That's a 1911 Honus Wagner baseball card, the famous T-206 card. Worth about $100,000.''

"What?" Joe blurted, meeting Frank's surprised gaze.

"Ssshhh!" McKay lifted an index finger to his lips, then looked up and down the counter at several customers milling about.

Frank also looked around, feeling suddenly secretive. Most of the browsers were busy shopping, but Frank noticed one man staring intensely at the trio at the counter. He was short and thin, with black wiry hair. His eyebrows were so thick that they seemed to stretch across his forehead in one bushy line.

When the man was aware that Frank had noticed him, he turned away quickly and walked out of the shop. Frank wondered how much of the conversation the man had heard.

"I knew it was valuable," Joe whispered, "but I didn't think it was worth *that* much."

"Well, it is," McKay stated with an emphatic nod.

Frank pointed down at the shelf beneath the glass countertop. "If it's so valuable, why do you have one sitting in your case?" he asked.

Joe looked down and saw that Frank was right. Sitting on the top shelf was an identical Honus Wagner card.

"That's a reprint," Mr. McKay explained. Unlocking the case, he pulled the reprint from the shelf. Holding both cards side by side, he said, "One of these cards is worth five bucks, and the other will make you rich. Can you guess which one is the original?"

Frank looked closely from one to the other for several seconds. At first glance they appeared identical, but then he saw that the colored tinting of the card in McKay's right hand was slightly duller than the coloring of the other card.

Pointing to the duller card, Frank said, "That one looks more authentic."

"Good eye," the old man said to Frank. "That's the one." He returned the card to the plastic sleeve and handed it to Frank.

"What makes this card so valuable?" Frank asked.

"Honus Wagner was one of the greatest short-stops the Pittsburgh Pirates ever had," McKay explained. "His plays were so incredible that they called him the Flying Dutchman. Even made the Hall of Fame, Wagner did." A warm glow came into McKay's eyes. Frank could see that the old man was in his element.

"Back in those days, baseball cards were originally put in pouches of tobacco and packages of cigarettes," McKay went on. "Kids loved to collect the cards. But Wagner didn't like the idea of kids buying cigarettes to get baseball cards and maybe smoking those cigarettes. The 1911 series is the only tobacco card featuring Honus Wagner because he refused to let the tobacco company put his picture on any more cards. In fact," McKay concluded, "Honus Wagner never had his picture on another card until the candy companies began selling the cards with bubble gum and other candy. That's why it's so valuable."

Frank let out a low whistle. Then he put the card in the inside pocket of his down jacket and pulled up the zipper. He suddenly felt very uncomfortable with the card resting near his heart.

"I still can't believe it's worth $100,000," Joe said.

Mr. McKay only shook his head. "There are only about fifty Wagner cards in existence today. I've been trying to get my hands on one for years."

"Well, thanks, Mr. McKay," Frank said. Turning to Joe, he said, "Let's get this home and put it in Dad's safe."

"If I were you, I'd even put it in a vault at the bank," Mr. McKay suggested.

"Good idea," Frank agreed with a laugh.

He and Joe said goodbye, then left the Old Ball Park.

The mall was packed with holiday shoppers, and Frank still felt uneasy. He knew it was ridiculous, but knowing the value of the card made him feel that everyone in the mall was aware that he had a $100,000 piece of cardboard riding in a plastic sleeve in the inside pocket of his jacket.

Once outside, Frank and Joe walked briskly to the van. A cold wind cut through the parking lot, whipping their cheeks. They had almost reached their vehicle when a loud voice boomed out beside them, "Happy holidays!"

Surprised, Frank spun to his right and found himself face-to-face with a big, beefy man. Frank guessed the guy's height to be somewhere around six feet four inches and his weight to be close to 300 pounds. Next to him was a shorter man—the man with wiry dark hair and the dark eyebrows that dominated his face who had been staring at them in the baseball shop!

The large man spoke again, his voice a deep, rumbling bass. "We're collecting for our favorite

11

charity. Would you two gents happen to have anything you would like to donate?"

"What charity is that?" Joe asked. His stance had become tense, and Frank could see that he, too, was ready for trouble from these goons.

"The Big Ben and Little Oscar charity," the big man answered.

The little man twisted his hand in a smooth motion. A split second later a switchblade knife appeared in it as if by magic, its silvery steel blade glinting in the sunlight.

Frank immediately jumped into a defensive crouch. Shooting a quick glance at the bigger man, he saw that the guy's right hand now held a long, black crowbar with a deadly pry hook on the end.

"Now," the big man said, smacking the crowbar against his beefy left hand, "do you want to give us the card, or do we have to cut and pry it out of you?"

Chapter

2

JOE TENSED in anticipation of the attack, coolly estimating the force of the big goon and his friend. Although Joe was a muscular six feet tall and his brother was an inch taller, the big guy looked to Joe to have twice the strength of either brother.

"Let's put them on ice now, Big Ben," the smaller man suggested, his bushy brows raised in excitement.

"We need to get the item first," Big Ben bellowed back.

"Hey," Joe cut in. "If you two are going to stand there yakking all afternoon, I think I'll be on my way."

Big Ben's dark eyes bulged with anger. "You're

13

hamburger, Hardy," he growled. Raising his right hand, he swung the crowbar straight at Joe's head.

Joe ducked beneath the slashing bar and slammed his right fist solidly into the center of Big Ben's oversize gut.

Big Ben jerked forward and dropped to his knees, clutching at his stomach and gasping for breath. The crowbar clattered to the asphalt pavement, and Joe kicked it away from the big man, then checked over his shoulder to see how Frank was doing.

The moment Big Ben had made his move on Joe, Oscar had jabbed at Frank's chest with the switchblade. But Frank had been ready. Taking a few steps backward, he lashed out with a cross kick that sent the knife flying from Oscar's hand. A look of amazed confusion came over Oscar's face as the knife sailed away from him, hit the ground, and spun under a car.

Frank grabbed Oscar by his jacket and pulled him up so the two stood nose to nose.

Frank's voice was low and threatening. "Now, would you mind explaining yourself before I push your teeth to the back of your skull?"

Oscar's eyes widened in fear. He opened his mouth to speak but was interrupted by the screaming blast of a car horn.

Frank jerked his head to the side in time to see a light green sedan bearing down on him and

Oscar. Just in time, Frank shoved Oscar away from him and jumped back in the opposite direction. Frank's push left Oscar sprawled on the ground. The car raced through the gap between Frank and Oscar, missing both of them by only a few inches.

"What the—" Frank heard the car pull to a stop. He didn't have time to see who it was, however, because from the corner of his eye, Frank saw Big Ben getting to his feet.

"Watch your back!" Frank yelled to his brother just as Big Ben swung his large right arm. Joe whirled around. He tried to dodge the roundhouse right, but Big Ben's fist was already speeding toward him. It caught Joe squarely on the hipbone, knocking him to the side and down.

Joe's face twisted in a grimace as the pain shot through his side. As quickly as he could, he rolled himself to a crouching position, ready to defend himself against the next onslaught.

Apparently Big Ben had other ideas. With one hand the big goon grabbed the back of Oscar's jacket collar and pulled the smaller man up. In the next moment the pair was running away from the Hardys at top speed. Before Joe and Frank could sprint after them their attackers jumped into a white BMW and squealed out of the mall parking lot.

"You okay?" Frank asked.

Joe grinned up at his brother. "Sure. I always

feel great after being pounded by a sledgehammer." He straightened up and was gingerly rubbing his left hip when a voice rang out nearby.

"Hey, Frank!" Frank and Joe turned and saw that someone was calling to them from the green sedan that had almost hit Frank and Oscar.

Frank saw a tall, lanky, dark-haired young man step from the driver's side of the car and start toward him and his brother.

It took Frank a moment, but then he remembered where he knew the guy from. Billy Murphy was also a senior at Bayport High. He had moved to Bayport during the previous spring semester, but Frank didn't know much else about him. Billy kept to himself. In fact, if Billy wasn't in Frank's computer and calculus classes, Frank wouldn't even know his name.

"You parked it a little close there, buddy," Joe said as Billy joined them.

"Pardon me?" Billy asked in a shy, quiet voice.

"We thought you were going to run us down," Frank said. "Don't mind my brother. It's just that he hates to lose."

"Sorry if I got in the way," Billy said. "When I saw those two with the crowbar and knife, I assumed you needed help." Billy cleared his throat. "Sorry," he repeated.

Joe rubbed his side. "That's okay."

"What did they want?" Billy asked.

"We didn't find out." Frank didn't like lying to Billy, but he didn't think it would be a good idea to mention the Honus Wagner card.

Billy glanced at his watch. "Oh—hey, I've got to go to work." He smiled at Frank. "Every time I go to the mall, I end up late to work."

Frank stared at Billy, a fresh interest in his brown eyes. "Where do you work?" he demanded.

"I work for my grandfather at the Bayport All Sports Stadium," Billy answered.

Frank nodded. He remembered hearing that Billy was the grandson of the new general manager of the Blues, Bayport's Triple-A minor league baseball club. The All Sports Stadium was the home of the Blues.

"What can you do at a baseball stadium in the off season?" Joe asked, giving Billy a curious glance.

"Anything Grandfather tells me to do," Billy said with a shrug.

"Sounds like our dad," said Frank.

"Right now I'm helping the equipment manager get some of the stuff ready for the next season. You wouldn't believe how those guys abuse all that expensive training equipment. I mean, they're supposed to be grown men who know better. I'd better get going. See ya." Billy gave them a quick wave, then walked back to the green sedan. He hopped into the car, backed

17

it away from the Hardys, and pulled out of the parking lot.

Frank's eyes followed the sedan out of the parking lot, but his mind was already on something else.

"I didn't get the license plate," he mumbled.

"What?" asked Joe.

"The BMW our two friends were driving. I didn't get the license plate number."

"I guess we were distracted by Billy coming up," Joe said. "Talk about bad timing."

Frank started for the van, his brow knit in concentration. Bad timing, yes, he thought. But was it deliberate?

"I don't get it, Frank," said Joe, breaking into Frank's thoughts. "How did those two know about the card?" Joe opened the driver's side door of the van and climbed behind the wheel while Frank got in the other side.

"I saw that Oscar guy checking us out while Mr. McKay was examining the card," Frank said, closing the van door. "I figured he was just curious at the time, but now that I think of it, he left in a hurry when he saw me looking at him."

Joe steered the van through the parking lot. "Yeah? Well, his curiosity has just bought him and his big friend trouble."

Frank and Joe stopped for some pizza on the

way home and talked about how they could track down the thugs.

"It's obvious that the two men want the card," Frank said between bites. "But who sent the card? And why?"

"Do you think there is a connection between whoever sent the card and the two thugs, or was their appearance at the mall just coincidental?" Joe asked his brother.

Frank shook his head and shrugged.

By the time Joe guided the van into the Hardys' driveway he and Frank had come up with twenty more questions, but neither of them had any answers.

They were glad to get out of the chilly afternoon air and into the warmth of the house. After hanging up his jacket in the hall closet, Frank pulled the baseball card from his inner pocket and looked again at the photo of Honus Wagner in his old-fashioned uniform.

He still couldn't believe that someone had sent him a faded piece of cardboard worth $100,000. Whoever had sent it to him either had to be crazy or had made a big mistake. Or both.

Frank tapped the card with his index finger. "I'm going to ask Dad about this," he announced.

He walked through the family room, down a hallway, and into Fenton Hardy's study. The sun had dipped low in the sky, and the study was shrouded with dark shadows. Frank didn't notice the dark form lying on the rug until he had almost tripped over it. Startled, he bent over and saw the body lying there, wearing the familiar white dress shirt and gray slacks, a trickle of dark red blood snaking down his temple.

Frank gasped. "Dad!"

Chapter

3

FOR HALF A SECOND Frank could only stare in horror at his father's immobile body. Then he knelt down beside Fenton and checked for a pulse, letting out a sigh of relief when he felt a strong one.

A moment later Fenton groaned and opened his eyes. Frank was gently helping him to his feet when Joe raced in.

"What happened?" Joe asked breathlessly. He ran to their father's other side. "Dad, are you all right?"

The two boys helped their father into the kitchen. As Fenton sat down at the table, Joe grabbed a towel, wet it with cold water, and handed it to him.

"Two men came to the door and said they wanted to hire me for a case," Fenton said slowly. He paused, grimacing as he touched the towel to his temple, then went on. "I explained to them that I couldn't possibly get to their problem until after the holidays. I was about to escort them out the door when the big one hit me with a blackjack."

"Was the big guy *really* big, and did he call himself Ben?" Frank asked, sitting on one of the other kitchen chairs.

Fenton looked at Frank in surprise. "Yes, but how did you know?"

"And the little guy was scrawny, didn't talk much, had one long eyebrow stretching across his forehead?" Joe interrupted.

Fenton nodded. "How did you know?"

"We had a run-in with them at the mall about an hour ago," Joe explained.

"And so you sent them to me so I wouldn't miss out on the fun?" Fenton said with a wry smile. He pressed the towel to his head again, and when he removed it, Frank saw a reddish blue bruise swelling on his left temple. "Did they say what they wanted?" Fenton asked.

"This." Frank took the Honus Wagner card from his pocket and handed it to his father.

"So *that's* what happened to it!" Fenton exclaimed, taking the card.

"What do you mean?" Joe asked.

"I was expecting this card about two hours ago," Fenton explained. He looked quizzically at his two sons. "What are you doing with it?"

"I thought it was for me," Frank told him. "The package was labeled 'F. Hardy.' "

"You're not the only one around here whose first name starts with an *F*," Fenton said with a laugh.

Frank gave his father an apologetic look. "Sorry."

"Well, who's it from?" Joe asked.

"Do you two know Stuart Murphy, the manager of the Blues?" Fenton questioned his sons.

"Not personally," Frank answered. "But I know his grandson."

"In fact, we just saw Billy at the mall. He kind of helped us with Ben and Oscar."

Helped us? Or helped *hurt* us? Frank wondered. It seemed like too much of a coincidence that Billy had just happened to be at the mall when the thugs had tried to steal a card that just happened to belong to Billy's grandfather.

"What's the connection between Mr. Murphy and the card?" Frank asked Fenton.

A hard, serious expression came over Fenton's face. "Someone's skimming money off the ticket sales and the sales at the concession stands," he began. "And Stuart Murphy's been told by the owner to find out who and how or lose his job."

"Is Mr. Murphy a suspect?" Frank asked.

"I think so," Fenton told them. "But Bob Barry, the owner of the Blues, doesn't want to come right out and accuse anyone until he has some proof."

Joe leaned back against the kitchen counter and crossed his arms over his chest. "So why has Murphy hired you?" he asked.

"Murphy is new to the club," Fenton explained. "He's only been with the Blues for one season, and he's still not sure whom he can trust. Anyone could be siphoning off funds, so Murphy wants an outside investigator, someone who doesn't have an interest in covering up the scandal."

Frank nodded. "Why the card?"

Fenton picked up the card from the kitchen table and looked at it. "After I interviewed Murphy, I told him I'd take the case, but that I wouldn't be able to get to it until after the holidays. He was very insistent and even went so far as to offer a retainer. I refused. He called me last night and said he was sending the card anyway, via courier. The card is a retainer."

"That's a pretty expensive retainer," Frank put in. "Even for someone who's desperate."

"Makes you think, doesn't it?" Joe added, a note of suspicion in his voice.

Frank nodded. He knew exactly what his brother meant. He'd be willing to bet someone was trying to get the card from Mr. Murphy, especially since Big Ben and his sidekick had been willing to bash his and Joe's heads in to get it.

But when Frank suggested as much to their father, Fenton shook his head. "I don't want to jump to any conclusions so early in the case. Murphy's anxious to find out who's embezzling from the club before Barry fires him." Fenton laid the card back on the table. "I suppose sending me the card is his way of telling me how important it is to him to clear his name. I'm going to give it back to him, of course. I can't see keeping something that's so valuable to him."

"Hey, why don't Joe and I help you on the case?" Frank suggested. He looked at his brother. "We could look for possible leads until you get back on Saturday."

"That's not a bad idea," Fenton said. Catching the wide grins on his sons' faces, he added, "Of course, this isn't your case, and I want you boys to be careful. And since this is my case, if you find anything, be sure to call me right away."

"You bet," said Frank.

"Good. I'll call Murphy and fill him in," Fenton said, reaching for the kitchen phone.

Joe carefully guided the van through the chain-link gate to the parking lot of the Bayport All Sports Stadium, which was located on the northwest edge of Bayport. He and Frank had been to dozens of games at the stadium—the Blues were one of the more successful Triple-A franchises and were often in the running for the Triple-A crown—but now Joe felt as if he were looking at it for the first time.

The seventeen thousand–seat stadium had been home to the minor league club for some twenty-five years, he knew. It was shaped like a horseshoe, and giant billboards around the outfield fence advertised various Bayport businesses.

Joe drove across the huge parking lot and pulled into a spot marked "Reserved."

"I don't think anybody will care," he said in reply to Frank's questioning look. "After all, it *is* the middle of winter."

They hopped from the van and headed toward the stadium's entrance gates, which, Joe noticed, were open and unguarded. They were at the back of the stadium, just outside a large cinderblock structure that curved around the outside of the seating and rose three stories in the air. The building was painted blue and white— the Blues' colors. Even though Joe couldn't see the seats or the field, he knew they were on the other side of the cinder-block building, along with the special glassed-in boxes for reporters and season-ticket holders.

Fenton had explained that the team's administrative offices were in the concrete structure. Stuart Murphy's office was on the third floor.

Joe and Frank passed through the gates and walked through a wide hallway that served as a concession area during games. Several concession stands, now closed for the off season, dotted the area. As he walked down the hall Joe noticed the ramps that led out to the seats. Boy, I can't wait until the season starts, Joe thought.

They had no trouble finding the elevator or getting to the third floor, and Joe was surprised at the ease with which they moved through the building. During game days, he recalled, the place was usually crawling with security, and fans were restricted to the seating and concession areas.

They worked their way down the musty-smelling hallway, their footsteps echoing in the empty space, until they found an open door labeled "General Manager." Joe and Frank entered the office.

"Hold it!" a voice shouted.

Joe froze as a blinding explosion of white light forced him to close his eyes. Temporarily disoriented, he stood still and blinked.

"Hey! What's the big deal?" he asked, rubbing his eyes.

"Uh-oh," a young woman's voice said. "Sorry. I thought you were someone else."

Red circles floated and swirled in front of Joe's eyes as he tried to readjust to the normal light of the room. He was about to yell at the person who had temporarily blinded him, but when his vision had cleared, he got a good look at the young woman who had fired the photo flash.

Joe couldn't tell how tall she was because she was sitting behind a black metal office desk, but he did notice her warm brown eyes, her collar-length red hair, and the few freckles that dotted her cheeks and nose. She looked to be about eighteen.

He stumbled up to the desk. "That's okay," Joe said, flashing her a brilliant smile. "I'm Joe Hardy, and this is my brother, Frank. We have an appointment with Mr. Murphy."

"I'm really sorry about the flash," the young woman repeated. She stood up, and Joe estimated her height to be around five foot six. She held out her right hand. "I'm Heather Hammons."

"My pleasure," said Joe, lightly gripping her hand.

"Mr. Murphy's been expecting you two." Heather moved to an inner office door that had Mr. Murphy's name on it. She opened the door and said, "Frank and Joe Hardy are here, Portside."

"Portside?" Joe repeated under his breath.

"Remember what Dad told us? He was a left-handed pitcher years ago," Frank answered.

Joe had been so preoccupied with the pretty redhead that he'd forgotten the briefing their father had given them before leaving for New York the night before. "I knew that," he said.

"Yeah, sure," Frank said with a smile.

A moment later the Hardys found themselves in Stuart Murphy's office. Frank looked casually around the big room, which looked quite comfortable for an office. There was a couch against one wall, a coffee machine on top of a long, low oak cabinet, and some trophies and signed photographs displayed on the shelves and on the wall. A big desk stood in front of the wall opposite the door, which was really a big expanse of windows. Frank guessed the windows overlooked the baseball diamond, even though blinds were drawn over them.

The tall, gray-haired man said hello and stepped from behind the desk. In a blue sports jacket and plaid slacks he looked trim and muscular for a man in his fifties.

"I'm Frank Hardy," Frank said. "And this is Joe."

"Did your father tell you everything?" Mr. Murphy asked after gesturing for them to take a seat on the couch. He rubbed the palms of his hands together anxiously, like a pitcher handling a baseball.

He sure seems upset, Frank thought. He's not wasting a second getting down to business.

"Yes," Frank said. "At least what you've told him so far. Someone's skimming money off the ticket and concession sales, and you've got a deadline for finding out who or you get canned."

"Bluntly put," Murphy said with a short nod. "I like that."

"Is there anything else we should know?" asked Frank.

Murphy walked to the large windows and peered through the pencil-thin slits in the wooden blinds. "First, I'd like to know what you two think you can do. I've got a lot riding on finding out who's embezzling the money."

"The card, for example?" Joe guessed.

All Murphy said was, "That's part of it." Then he was silent. Murphy didn't turn around, but Frank thought he detected a certain nervousness.

"And the other part?" Frank prompted. For someone who wanted to solve a crime, Murphy sure seemed reluctant to share the facts.

Murphy turned to face the Hardys, his hands in his pockets. "What do you know about me?"

Frank rattled off the list of information their father had given them.

"You used to pitch for the Kansas City Athletics before they moved to Oakland. You were known as Portside Murphy, the left-hander with the meanest slider in the majors, and were even considered future Hall of Fame material. Then a line drive caught you in the elbow and shattered the joint, ending your career when you were only twenty-two. Since then you've been managing and coaching up and down the sandlot circuit and the major league teams. Your last stop before ending up in Bayport was with the Oklahoma City Cavalry. But you were fired without explanation about a year ago."

Mr. Murphy seemed impressed. "You've done your homework, I'll give you that. But can you help me find the creep who's stealing the money and making my life impossible? You're just kids."

"Our father is running the case, Mr. Murphy," Frank explained. "We're just the designated hitters until he returns on Saturday."

Frank didn't bother to add that he and Joe had solved dozens of cases, and that the Bayport police had even solicited their aid on several occasions.

"So," Joe said, "this could be the last inning in your baseball career."

Mr. Murphy sat down in the leather chair behind his desk, then looked from Frank to Joe. After a long silence he finally said, "You're right. I'm through in baseball if I'm fired from this job. I wouldn't even be able to get a job coaching five-year-olds in some tee-ball league."

Frank leaned forward on the couch. He and Joe needed a lot more to go on before they could get started on the case. "Why were you fired from your last job?" Frank asked.

"Who's to say?" Murphy replied with a shrug. "Owners can do as they please."

"You mean you didn't question being fired?" Frank asked.

Murphy turned and leaned on the desk. "I accepted the firing because that was preferable to being accused of something I didn't do."

"And what was that?" Joe asked.

Murphy sighed. "The Cavalry was showing promise at the start of the season. As a new team, it wasn't expected to finish much higher than last. But we put on a run that I thought might take us all the way to the World Series."

"I remember," said Frank, nodding. "You went into the second half of the season in second place, behind Kansas City, and then finished the season dead last."

"Don't remind me," Murphy said, grimacing. "The owner of the team accused me of fixing the lineup, rigging it so that the batting order was weak and we'd lose games." His voice was tinged with bitterness. "He actually claimed I was gambling, betting against my own team."

Frank stared at the older man. He knew that gambling was illegal in all but a few states. And gambling on your own team was a serious conflict of interest. "Did you bet on sports?" Frank asked, deciding to take a direct approach.

"Sure, legally. But never on baseball games, and certainly not against my own team." Mr. Murphy's face reddened. "Say, whose side are you on? If this is the way you plan on helping me, you boys can get out my office right now."

Frank held up his hands. "We're just here to look for evidence."

"Right. Uh, sorry."

"You could answer another question for us, Mr. Murphy," Joe said. "Why did you send such an expensive card to our father by courier? Didn't you realize the risk you were taking?"

At that question Murphy became agitated, fumbling with his words before he finally sputtered, "It was the only way I could convince your father how important this is to me. I've had that card since I was ten. Won it in a melon-seed-spitting contest. I plan on passing it along to Billy someday. Would have given it to his father, but, well . . . he and Billy's mother died five years ago in a car accident."

"We didn't know," Frank said in a sympathetic tone.

"If I lose this job, I'm finished in baseball. I don't think I could face Billy then. If anything good comes out of that card, it's that Billy has a ticket to college or a good start at whatever he wants in life."

Murphy leaned back in his chair and rubbed his eyes. "Okay. Here's what's been happening. I arrived here last March and took over operations. As you know, the Blues had a hot season. Gate attendance was up, which means that concession receipts should also have been up. But Mr. Barry learned from his accountants last week that the gate attendance and concession receipts were short—to the tune of $150,000."

"Wow!" Joe exclaimed.

"And Mr. Barry suspects you took the money?" Frank guessed.

Murphy nodded. "He didn't come right out and say it in so many words, but I could tell what he was hinting at. He kept mentioning the trouble I had with the Cavalry." Murphy gave the Hardys a hard stare. "And that's the whole story. Now, what can you guys do to help?"

"We've got a plan," Frank began. "You take Joe and me on as extra help. I'll work in the accounting section, where I'll have access to the computers. I'm pretty sure that whoever is embezzling the money is doing it electronically. Joe can work odd jobs, see what he can pick up by roaming freely."

"Sounds good to me," Mr. Murphy said. He thought for several moments, his brow furrowed. "You realize that Billy will know why you two are here?"

"Yes," Frank said. "You need to tell him to keep quiet so Joe and I can work undercover."

"Okay, you can start tomorrow." Mr. Murphy stood, indicating that their meeting was over.

"We'll do our best," Frank said as he and Joe rose and shook the older man's hand.

"I hope that's good enough," Murphy said in a tired voice.

Frank and Joe walked out of the office, leaving Murphy to stare out through the blinds.

"I don't think he's told us everything," Frank said as he and Joe rode the elevator down to the ground floor.

"I know what you mean," Joe agreed. "His explanation was too compact, too neat. Almost sounded as if it was rehearsed."

The elevator doors opened, and the Hardys stepped out into the large concession area that curved around the ground floor of the stadium.

A slight movement caught Joe's eye, and he turned to smile when he spotted Heather's slender silhouette in the fluorescent light. She was fifty yards away, loading film into her camera.

"Hey, Heather!" Joe called out, and he headed over to her. He followed her onto the baseball field, allowing himself to imagine what it would be like to be in the stadium not as a fan, but as a baseball star, one who would impress a certain attractive photograper.

He glanced at Heather but did a double take when he saw the sudden change in her expression. Her smile disappeared, and her brown eyes opened wide with fear.

"Joe!" she shouted. "Look out!"

Joe spun around too late.

Three baseballs were rocketing straight for his head!

Chapter

4

JOE DIDN'T HAVE TIME to duck. His arms flew instinctively in front of his face—and not a moment too soon. Two of the baseballs struck his shoulder while the third slammed into his left collarbone, flinging him backward. Joe let out a cry of pain and fell to the ground.

Then the burning started—a slow, persistent heat that began in his left shoulder and crept up to the collarbone, where the fire exploded into an inferno of pain.

"Joe!" Frank's worried face appeared above him.

Joe groaned. "I think . . . my collarbone's . . . broken."

He tried to keep his left arm still. The burning

had worked its way down to his left fingers, but the ground beneath him was freezing. It was strange to feel hot and cold at the same time.

"I'll call an ambulance," Frank said, and he ran for the nearest phone.

"Are you okay, Joe?"

Joe turned his head enough to see that Heather had run up and was kneeling beside him. Her words were accented by the white puffs of air she exhaled into the cold stadium.

"Just enjoying the view," he quipped through gritted teeth as he looked up into Heather's clear brown eyes. "What happened?"

"Hey, I'm sorry," Joe heard someone call out.

A second later he saw Billy Murphy stroll up behind Heather, his hands in his pockets.

"I was working on the pitching machine and hit the button by accident," Billy explained. He pointed with his thumb down toward a big blue metal machine that stood about sixty feet away. Joe could hear its motor still humming.

Heather looked at Joe, her brown eyes full of worry. "When I saw the balls heading for you, I was terrified."

"It's a good thing you shouted," Joe said, trying to smile. "If you hadn't, they would have beaned me in the back of the skull."

The fire in his arm had subsided, but now a cold numbness was setting in. He knew it was probably the first signs of shock creeping up on him.

"Ambulance is on its way," Frank announced, returning to the group. He looked from Heather to Billy, then asked, "What happened?"

Billy explained about the pitching machine again. "I've been working on it all week, trying to get it to throw only one ball at a time. I was tightening a bolt, but my hand slipped, and it hit the switch. I should have checked to see if it was loaded. Sorry, Joe."

Joe looked at Billy. He might have said he was sorry with his voice, but his eyes registered something else—he couldn't tell if it was guilt or fear. If he had more strength, Joe would have confronted Billy and forced the truth out of him.

But Joe was in no condition to do anything but lie still and listen to the high-pitched whine of the ambulance siren as the emergency vehicle approached the stadium.

"This is going to be a great Christmas," Joe mumbled as he walked into the Hardy home.

His left arm rested in a shoulder sling. The collarbone had only been bruised, but Joe had to keep it immobile for at least four weeks. His left shoulder was swollen with large bruises where the other two balls had hit him.

Frank and Heather stepped into the house after him. "I'm just thankful your collarbone

39

wasn't broken,'' Heather said. She helped Joe take off his jacket and then hung it up in the hall closet.

Frank turned to Heather. "Thanks for driving us back from the hospital.'' Heather had followed Frank and the ambulance to the hospital in her car and then had driven Frank back to the stadium for the **van** once Joe had been released. Frank had invited her back for some hot cocoa.

"Why don't you guys have a seat?'' he said, gesturing toward the den. "I'll go make the cocoa.''

"You always carry your camera with you?'' Joe asked as he and Heather sat in the two lounge chairs.

"Always,'' Heather replied with a smile.

He cocked his head to one side. "I don't remember seeing you around Bayport High. You're not a student there, are you?''

"No.'' Heather brought her camera around and held it in front of her face, pointing it at Joe and focusing the lens. "I graduated from Southport High last year,'' she explained after a moment. Joe knew that Southport was about midway between Bayport and New York City.

Heather pressed the shutter release, and the camera fired off several shots, the auto-advance moving the film through the camera at lightning speed.

"You're wasting your film,'' Frank said, returning to the den with a tray of steaming cocoa. Ignoring his brother's indignant look, Frank presented the tray to Heather, who took two cups and handed one to Joe.

Sitting cross-legged on the den carpet, Frank asked Heather, "What are you doing at the All Sports Stadium?"

"Trying to make some money so I can go to college," Heather replied, sipping the cocoa. "Thanks, Frank. This is good. I want to major in design, but I don't have the money to get into a really good art school, so I'm working as a public relations intern."

"Sounds ambitious," Joe commented.

"I'm a good photographer," Heather said without modesty, "and an even better designer."

"It's great that you have so much confidence in yourself," Joe said. He sipped his cocoa, keeping his eyes locked on Heather's.

Oh, brother, Frank thought, rolling his eyes. Here we go again!

"But I'm not working for the Blues by accident. When I graduated from high school and heard that Stuart 'Portside' Murphy was general manager of the Blues, I begged for a job. I've been a baseball fan since I could sit up. I was yelling at umpires, eating hot dogs, and singing 'Take Me Out to the Ballgame' when most kids were learning to say 'mama.' How about you two?'' said Heather. ''What were you doing at the stadium?''

Frank quickly spoke up. ''Mr. Murphy's a friend of Dad's, and he's offered us a job during the holiday break.''

Heather put her cup down on the tray and stood up. ''Well, I've got to run,'' she said, smiling at Joe. ''Thanks for the cocoa. And I am sorry about your collarbone.''

''It wasn't your fault,'' Joe said. He, too, stood and then escorted Heather to the front door.

Frank shook his head as he followed his brother with his eyes. ''Look out,'' he mumbled to himself. ''Joe's in love again.''

Joe and Frank arrived at the All Sports Stadium bright and early Tuesday morning. A light drizzle had fallen the night before, covering the roads with a glassy coat of ice, but Frank had negotiated the slippery roads without trouble. Just before nine he eased the van through the stadium's entrance, parking in the same spot they had used the day before.

Joe had remained silent during the ride. With his bruised collarbone he wouldn't be able to do much more than pull files out of a drawer. It wouldn't be exciting work.

''Look at it this way,'' Frank told him as they rode the elevator to the third floor. ''You'll get to scan the files for any bogus concession receipts, and we can double check what you find against what the computer says."

"Thrillsville," Joe moaned.

Frank stopped in front of a door marked "Files," halfway down the third-floor hallway. "Here's your stop. See you at lunch."

"If I don't die of boredom first," Joe shot back. He opened the door.

"You're late," a grumbling voice greeted him. Joe let out a resigned sigh when he saw the woman sitting at a desk across the room. Her hair was a dull gray, like the winter sky, and she wore large square glasses too big for her small, angular face. She was pale, and she didn't smile.

The room had only one window, and its walls were lined with filing cabinets. Piles of papers were in bins on a table next to the woman's desk, no doubt just waiting for him to file them.

Great, Joe thought as he closed the door behind him.

Frank walked the length of the hallway to where the accounting office was. Just as he was about to push open the office door, he heard Mr. Murphy call, "Frank."

Turning, Frank saw Mr. Murphy and another man walking down the hallway toward him.

"I'd like you to meet Rocky Snyder," Mr. Murphy said. "Rocky, this is Frank Hardy."

The stocky man nodded, looking closely at Frank from blue eyes set deep in his square face. Snyder looked to be somewhere between forty-five and fifty, Frank guessed. He was as tall as Frank, but he was carrying twenty more pounds than he should have been.

"It's a pleasure," Frank said, grabbing the older man's hand. He was surprised at the strength in Snyder's grip.

"Rocky owns the Albany Governors, our rivals," Murphy explained. "The ones who beat us out of the Triple-A pennant race last year."

"We'll get you next season," Frank told Snyder with a smile.

"Not with Hard-Luck Murphy on your side." Rocky's laugh was heavy and deep.

"Never mind," Murphy said. "Excuse me, Rocky, while I talk to Frank for a minute."

"Sure," Rocky said with a smile. "I'll meet you back in your office." He walked down the hallway and disappeared into Murphy's office.

"He also owns Major League Concessions," Murphy told Frank. "They're our main supplier of food and merchandise for the concession stands."

"I'll remember that," Frank said, nodding. He and Joe would definitely check into the company for any connection to the concession embezzlement.

"Billy told me about the accident with the

pitching machine. I hope Joe's all right." Murphy clapped an arm around his shoulder. "I just wanted you to know I've given the regular data processor some extra vacation time so you'll have an opportunity to work alone."

"That'll help a lot," Frank said.

"Good. If you and your brother get me through this, you'll have season tickets to all Blues games for the rest of your lives."

"Thanks," Frank said as Murphy moved down the hallway to his office.

Frank opened the door to the accounting office and looked around. He was standing at one end of a small room that seemed even smaller than it was because it was so full. Three large desks with computer screens jutted out into the room, leaving little space in which to move around. Frank snaked his way to the largest terminal.

"Hello," he said to the computer as he turned it on. Sitting down in a swivel chair, he entwined his fingers and stretched his arms out in front of him, cracking his finger joints. "Let's see what secrets you have hidden within you."

For the first half hour, Joe moved one set of files from a blue filing cabinet to a black one, and then another set from the black cabinet to the blue one—a slow process with the use of only one arm. He tried to figure out what exactly it was that he was doing, but he didn't want to ask his supervisor—she'd told him her name was Mrs. Shaffer—and so continued the tedious task until he thought he would scream. Joe looked at every file he moved, but so far he hadn't seen anything having to do with tickets or concession sales.

There was at least one good thing, Joe thought, glancing over his shoulder. The office's one window looked down onto the baseball field. Looking out at the field every now and then helped to break up the monotony of the dull office and the duller job.

He was about to put the last pile of files in the bottom drawer of the blue cabinet when he glanced once more out the window.

His hand stopped in midair as he spotted Heather. She was on the field by third base, her camera in hand, her copper hair falling against the denim jacket she wore.

Joe didn't hesitate for a second. Grabbing his jacket with his good arm, he walked past Mrs. Shaffer's desk. "I'm taking a break," he announced, and then he swept out of the office before she could protest.

Moments later he walked up behind Heather. "Hello."

"Hey, Joe." She gave him a wide smile. "How's the collarbone?"

"Still in one piece. What are you taking pictures of?"

"Don't tell my boss," she said in a low voice. "I'm just getting some shots for myself."

"Stealing company time, huh?"

"You won't tell, will you?" Heather's face was serious.

"How could I when I'm doing the same thing myself." He reached for the camera with his right hand. "May I?"

"You sure you can handle it with one hand?" Heather asked, a skeptical look on her face. "That's a three-hundred-millimeter lens."

"No problem," Joe replied. Taking the camera, he hooked the strap around his neck and looked through the telephoto lens. "I'm taking a photography class at Bayport High. Got an A so far."

He panned the stadium, cradling the long lens in his palm and fingering the focus ring with his thumb and index finger. "This is a cool lens," he said. "Really brings faraway objects up close."

He had scanned over to his right and up into one of the corporate boxes. Two fuzzy, unfocused black objects caught his eye, so he adjusted the lens until they were crystal clear.

Joe blinked. Was he seeing right? Two guys were sitting in a box, apparently engaged in a heated argument. Joe recognized both of them, but he had a hard time accepting what he saw.

47

Reaching up with his index finger, Joe pressed the shutter release and fired off several shots with the automatic advance. He hoped Heather didn't mind him taking the pictures, but he wanted to show Frank and Mr. Murphy the photos.

Joe released the shutter again just to make sure he had proof that the two men arguing in the VIP box were Big Ben and Billy Murphy!

Chapter

5

"SO THIS IS WHERE you've been all morning."

Frank just about jumped out of his skin. For the past three hours, he had been so intensely focused on the computer terminal that he had shut out all other sights and sounds. He hadn't even heard the door to the accounting office open. And yet there she was, standing in the doorway. Callie Shaw's blond hair framed her pretty face, and her brown eyes sparkled.

"Man," Frank said with a gasp. "You scared me, Callie. My goose bumps have goose bumps."

"I missed you, too," she teased. She came into the office and shut the door. "I was on my way to the mall to do some Christmas shopping, but I saw the van out in the lot, so I decided to stop by. It's pretty empty around here, but I finally found someone who told me where you're working." She bent over the desk to look at the computer screen. "Trying to earn some cash for an extra-special holiday gift for an extra-special person?" she asked, smiling down at Frank.

"Yeah." Frank shot her a teasing glance. "My computer needs a disk drive."

"Oh, you're impossible!"

"That's why you like me so much," Frank returned.

"What are you doing here, Frank Hardy?"

Frank patted the top of the computer terminal and said mysteriously, "Secrets. Secrets hidden in plain sight. Secrets that could make a computer hacker cry with joy."

"Cut the dramatics." Callie rolled her eyes. "Really, what are you up to?"

Frank laughed. "Okay, here's the story." He quickly explained about Mr. Murphy's $100,000 baseball card and the embezzling from the Blues organization. He decided not to tell her about the fight with Big Ben and Oscar. It would only worry her.

"And I've found something very interesting," Frank concluded, running his fingers over the keyboard as he entered commands.

"What's that?" Callie asked.

Frank hit the Enter button, and the computer clicked and hummed. "This'll just take a minute.

I'm making a copy of this stuff for my computer at home. I want to double check my findings before I show them to Mr. Murphy."

Frank tapped his fingers on the desk. He was anxious to get the information copied. If word got around that he and Joe were investigating the embezzlement, someone could erase the valuable information that had been cleverly hidden in the computer. He still didn't know whom he and Joe could trust around the Blues organization.

"Let's go," Frank said as he flipped up the computer's disk drive and took out a plastic disk.

"Where to?" Callie asked, buttoning up her coat.

"How does pizza sound?" Frank asked. He put the disk in his shirt pocket, threw on his jacket, and zipped it up. "Come on. Let's find Joe."

Frank led Callie down the hallway to the file room and opened the door. Instead of Joe he saw the pale, angular face of a gray-haired woman whose large glasses gave her the appearance of a bug. She greeted Frank with a frown.

"Have you seen Joe?" Frank asked. "I'm his brother."

"He went to lunch with Ms. Hammons," Mrs. Shaffer said in a disapproving tone. "And he didn't finish filing these papers." She indicated a large stack of papers perched on the table next to her desk.

"Thanks," Frank said. He quickly shut the door, then whispered to Callie, "Talk about a cold reception. That woman could freeze out Old Man Winter!"

"Shhh!" said Callie, giggling. "Who's Ms. Hammons?"

"Joe's new romantic interest," Frank replied as they headed for the elevator.

Callie raised a brow. "Another one?"

"Looks that way."

A few minutes later they were in the van, heading out of the parking lot and toward the Bayport Mall pizza joint.

"So?" Callie said. "What big secrets have you found?"

"It's so simple that I can hardly believe someone had the nerve to try such a scheme," Frank began. "You see, the ticket sales and the gate count never matched up during the season."

"But—" Callie began.

"I know," Frank interrupted. "Ticket sales and gate counts wouldn't necessarily add up, because it's certain that some people who bought tickets didn't show up for the games. You would expect that ticket sales would outnumber the gate count. And on some home-game days that's exactly what happened."

"The important word being *'some,'*" Callie put in.

"Exactly," Frank replied with a smile. "But on most home-game days," he continued, "the gate count was *larger* than the ticket count. In other words—"

It was Callie's turn to interrupt. "More people showed up at the games than actually had tickets."

"Not exactly," Frank said. "All those people had tickets, and all the tickets were sold to them. But somebody programmed the computer to record only a certain number of tickets sold. For example . . ."

Frank paused as he slowed the van to stop at a red light. The streets were still slick, and he had to gently ease the van to a stop to prevent the wheels from locking up on the ice. As he waited he let out a big yawn.

The morning's work must have tired him, Frank thought. He'd have to be careful driving. Turning to Callie, he continued explaining. "Let's say that for one game the computer registered a total of five thousand tickets sold, but the gate count at the turnstiles said that five thousand one hundred twenty-two fans showed up."

"Maybe there's a problem with the turnstile," Callie suggested.

"With one or two turnstiles, maybe," Frank said. "But not all eight."

"I see what you mean. What kind of money are we talking about?"

Frank stepped on the gas pedal as the light turned green. "Let's assume on an average that the count is off by 122 fans," he said, stifling another yawn. "That's 122 tickets unaccounted for in the computer records. Now, an average ticket price is fifteen dollars."

"That's eighteen hundred dollars!" Callie blurted out.

"Eighteen hundred and thirty dollars, to be exact," Frank corrected. "With fifty home games this past season, that comes to a grand total of over ninety-one thousand dollars. And that's just part of what's missing. I haven't even gotten to the concession scam yet," Frank continued. "I'm hoping Joe can pull up some paperwork that I can compare to my computer notes."

He yawned. Then he noticed Callie yawning, too. Must be contagious, he thought.

His eyes were feeling heavier and heavier. He blinked and shook his head, but he felt as if he were moving in slow motion. Why am I so tired? he asked himself.

As if through a mental haze, Frank saw the traffic light up ahead, its green eye slowly changing to yellow, and then to red. Cars pulled out into the intersection from the busy cross street.

Frank took his foot off the accelerator. At

least, he tried to lift his foot from the accelerator, but his foot was heavy, like lead.

He turned groggily toward Callie and saw that her head was tilted back against the headrest and her eyes were closed. She was asleep.

Slowly Frank forced his attention back to the street. Everything seemed to slow down—everything except the rushing traffic in the intersection. Again he tried to lift his foot, and this time he managed to drag it off the gas pedal. The haze in front of Frank's eyes grew denser. He was vaguely aware of a dry, burned odor like burning car oil.

As he approached the intersection, a terrifying thought swam to the surface of Frank's consciousness.

He wasn't tired from any natural cause. He was slowly being choked to death by carbon monoxide fumes!

Chapter

6

A LOUD, SHARP SCREAM yanked Frank from the deep sleep in which he had been so peacefully resting.

He lifted his head, his eyes straining to see through the gray haze in front of him. Then it hit him: The scream was a car's blaring horn.

Frank's eyes popped open, and he saw that the van was smack in the middle of the busy intersection. Cars were veering wildly to avoid hitting him.

Somehow he managed to gently push down on the brakes, let up, and push down again. The van slowed, veering to the right as its wheels slid on the icy road. At last it bumped up on the curb and came to a halt.

Reaching down, Frank threw the van's gear shift into park and shut off the engine. He was barely aware of the group of pedestrians that had crowded around them, yelling angrily at Frank. All he could think about was getting out of the deadly van.

He opened his door and stumbled out, falling to the street on his hands and knees. A severe pounding echoed between his ears and tried to push itself out through his temples. Gripping the door to steady himself, he got to his feet and made his way unsteadily around to the other side of the van.

Someone asked him if he was okay, but the pounding in his head was so bad he couldn't answer. He breathed deeply, letting the fresh air clear his head. By the time he pulled open the passenger door, Frank felt steady enough to lower Callie to the sidewalk without falling himself. Cradling her face in his hands, he gently shook it.

"Callie," he said softly.

She didn't answer. Her face was white, and her lips almost blue. Frank lifted one eyelid. Callie's eye was turned up so only the white was showing.

"Do you need help?" a young woman asked.

Frank swallowed his fears for Callie. He knew he had to stay in control if he was going to help her. "In the . . . van," Frank said slowly, pointing to the open passenger door. "Phone. Dial star-911. We need an ambulance."

As the woman hurried to the van, Frank began mouth-to-mouth resuscitation. At first Callie didn't respond. But after a few moments, she groaned, then coughed. The color began to return to her lips and face.

Then she coughed again and opened her eyes, and Frank let out a deep sigh of relief.

"I didn't realize you were so interested in photography, Joe," Heather said.

Joe turned to her and smiled. "It's the least I could do for shooting up all of your film. I didn't realize that the shutter release was so sensitive."

Heather was leaning against the counter that ran along one wall of the small room on the third floor of the stadium that served as her darkroom. Behind her was a deep sink, and on the counter were several trays with chemicals in them. The rest of the room held storage drawers, shelves with bottles of chemicals and photographic paper, a light box, and a drying rack with clips, all of which were bathed in the golden amber of the darkroom's safe light.

"I had the auto-advance set for five frames a second. Too high," Heather told him. "It's as much my fault as yours."

Joe had developed the negatives, and he was now making a print of one of the many shots he had taken of Billy and Big Ben in the VIP box.

"You still haven't told me why you want a print from those negs you shot," Heather said.

"Well," Joe began, keeping his voice calm, "my photography teacher said we had to put together a portfolio during the Christmas break. This means I'll have one less picture to worry about."

"I don't want to hurt your feelings, Joe," Heather said as she eyed the print that was soaking in the developing solution, "but that's a pretty dull shot to include in a portfolio."

"I guess."

Joe didn't like lying to Heather. But what could he say? That Big Ben and Oscar might be involved in an embezzling scam, and that Billy's presence with Big Ben made *him* suspicious, too? Joe wasn't planning to tell her about the case.

Using plastic tongs, Joe lifted the eight-by-ten print from the developing solution and put it in a tray labeled "Stop Bath" for ten seconds, which slowed down the developing process. Then, lifting the photo again, he gently flicked off the excess chemical and put the print in a third tray, marked "Fixer," to neutralize both the developing and stop bath chemicals and "fix" the print so that white light would not affect it.

"Ready?" Heather asked after the print had been in the fixer for about fifteen seconds.

"Yeah," Joe said, wiping his hands on a paper towel while she flicked on the overhead light. He blinked until his eyes had adjusted somewhat to the bright light.

"You know," Heather said, hopping down from the counter, "I can think of about a zillion subjects more interesting than Big Ben Norman and Billy Murphy standing in a VIP box at the All Sports Stadium."

"You know Big Ben?" Joe asked, eyeing Heather.

She shrugged. "I guess. He's been hanging around the stadium for a few weeks. But to tell you the truth, I don't really know what he's doing here." Heather folded her arms across her chest. "You know Big Ben?"

"No," Joe said, shaking his head. "I just need a name for the portfolio." He decided to play a hunch. "Didn't I see him earlier with a short guy? You know, the one with one eyebrow?" Joe drew an imaginary eyebrow across his forehead.

"Yeah," Heather replied. "That's Oscar, Big Ben's gofer. You know: go for this, go for that. Speaking of which," she added, a sparkle in her brown eyes, "I could go for some lunch. I'm famished."

"Me, too," Joe said. Maybe he could find out more about Big Ben and Oscar while they ate.

The print had been in the fixer for about three minutes. Not the recommended time, Joe thought, but long enough to keep the print from fading anytime soon. Taking the print from the tray, he tossed it into a tray beneath the tap, ran some water over it, shook off the excess water, then hung it up to dry.

Just as he opened the darkroom door and stepped out into the third-floor hallway, he heard Mr. Murphy's booming voice.

"There you are!"

Joe could sense the urgent note in the voice, and when he turned, he saw an unmistakable look of fear in the older man's eyes.

"What's wrong, Mr. Murphy?" Joe asked.

"It's—it's your brother and his girlfriend," Mr. Murphy stammered. "They've been in an accident!"

Heather drove Joe to the hospital, and they sat in the waiting area outside the emergency room while Frank and Callie were being examined by a physician. Frank and Callie looked pale and shaken up when they finally emerged from the examination room with the doctor, but Joe was relieved to see that there didn't seem to be any serious injury. After instructing Frank and Callie to stay a little while for observation, the doctor left.

"What happened?" Joe asked in a rush.

"We sucked in about a gallon of carbon monoxide," Frank told him. "One minute we were wide awake, and the next thing I knew I had straddled the van on a curb."

Joe caught the intense look his brother gave him, which told him he would hear the rest of Frank's story when they were in private. "I'll drive you home as soon as the doc says it's okay," Joe said.

"Yeah, right," Heather said skeptically, pointing at his sling. "You've got one good wing, and you think you're going to be able to drive them home?"

"It was a thought," Joe said, looking at his brother and shrugging. "Would you mind playing chauffeur again, Heather?"

"No . . ." she said slowly. "Not if you two would tell me what's going on." Heather stood with her arms crossed, her eyebrows raised expectantly.

"What do you mean?" Joe tried to sound casual, but he knew by the frown on Heather's face that he wasn't very convincing.

"First of all," Heather began, "I may not have been in Bayport long, but I know who you two are."

"You do?" Joe asked, surprised.

"Sure. You remember the chop-shop ring you busted in Southport last spring?" Heather asked.

Joe nodded, remembering the time he had almost lost his best friend, Chet Morton, to a ruthless car thief.

"So are you two investigating the embezzlement scam or not?" Heather asked bluntly.

Joe just stared at her, taken aback. Before he could open his mouth, Frank came forth with the question that had sprung to Joe's mind.

"What do you know about it?" Frank asked.

"Just what Billy has told me," Heather answered. "If his grandfather doesn't find out who's taking the money, Barry'll fire him."

"Billy's supposed to keep this operation a secret," Frank said.

"Well, he told me you two were investigating the scam," Heather responded. "He knows he can trust me."

"This is getting very interesting," Joe said. If Billy had told Heather about their investigation, had he told Big Ben, too?

"What do you mean?" Heather asked.

"Yes, why?" Callie chimed in.

Joe looked at the girls, then shrugged. Since they already knew about the case, he might as well be direct. "I've got photographic evidence of a meeting between Big Ben and Billy," he told them.

"A picture?" Frank asked. "Where?"

"Heather's darkroom at the stadium."

"Let's take a look at it," Frank said.

Frank and Callie told a nurse that they felt fully recovered and then signed some papers to check out of the hospital.

"What about the van?" Joe asked. "Where is it?"

Frank explained that the van had been left parked downtown. "First we'll get some lunch, then we can pick the van up on the way to the stadium."

As Heather drove, Joe's mind was racing, trying to piece together the connection between Billy, Big Ben, the card, and the scam. Obviously there was some connection between Big Ben and Billy, but could Billy be trying to hurt his own grandfather?

When they reached the intersection where the van was, Joe still hadn't made sense of the facts. Pulling himself back to the situation at hand, Joe knelt down at the rear of the van and peeked underneath. He steadied himself, reached behind the rear tire with his right arm, and yanked out a section of green tubing that looked as if it had been cut from a garden hose.

"Someone ran this from the exhaust pipe to a hole in the floor next to the wheel well," Joe explained, holding up the hose. "That's why you guys inhaled those carbon monoxide fumes. The van's safe to drive now.''

"I'll drive,'' Frank said, pulling the keys from his jacket pocket. "But just to be on the safe side, Callie can ride with Heather.'' Frank looked at Heather. "I mean, if you don't mind.''

"Not at all,'' Heather said. "Things were getting a little boring around the stadium until you two showed up,'' she added, grinning. "Come on, Callie.''

"I'd better ride with Frank,'' Joe said.

Fifteen minutes later they all met in the parking lot of the stadium, and Heather led the way to the third-floor darkroom.

Joe hesitated as they reached the door, which was wide open. "Hey, didn't you lock the door?''

"Yeah, right when we left for the hosp—'' Heather stopped short, and a look of dismay came over her face.

"No!'' she screamed.

Joe looked over her shoulder and into the darkroom. It had been completely torn apart. Boxes of photographic paper had been ripped open and exposed to the light, making the expensive paper unusable. Photos that Heather had used to decorate the walls were torn down and shredded. The floor was littered with ripped negatives.

Stepping around Heather, Joe raced into the

darkroom and began frantically searching among the torn photos and negatives. After a moment he threw up his hands.

"They're gone," he announced angrily. "All the negatives and the only print of Big Ben and Billy are gone!"

Chapter

7

FRANK STARED at the mess in the darkroom, then turned to his brother. "Who do you think did it?"

Joe didn't appear to hear the question. Snapping his fingers, he mumbled, "There's something I want to check out."

He raced back out of the vandalized darkroom and headed down the wide passageway toward the elevators.

"What's up?" Frank asked as he, Callie, and Heather caught up with Joe and rode the elevator down.

"Testing out a theory," Joe replied. When they got to the stadium floor, Joe ran outside to the pitching machine and began tinkering with it.

"Just as I thought," he announced a minute later. He pointed at the area around the on-off switch. "There's no bolt, screw, or nut anywhere near the switch. The closest bolt is this half-inch on the opposite side of the machine. Billy couldn't have slipped and accidentally hit the on switch. He had to do it deliberately." Joe flipped the machine on. It hummed to life, and the big pitching wheel began spinning.

"Watch out," Frank warned.

"Nothing happens when you turn the machine on," Joe explained. "You've got to feed the baseballs into the machine, then it pitches them wherever you aim the pitching arm."

"You mean Billy deliberately had the machine throw those balls at you?" Heather asked, shock registering in her voice.

"Yes," Joe said matter-of-factly.

Frank turned to Heather. "Someone obviously knew about the photos Joe had taken of Big Ben and Billy. Any ideas?"

"No," Heather replied after a moment.

"What about Mr. Murphy?" prompted Joe. "He could have seen the photo hanging up to dry when I opened the door."

"That's possible," Frank said.

Heather shook her head. "Why would he want to destroy the print and all the negatives?" she demanded.

"To protect his grandson," answered Joe.

68

"Or perhaps Big Ben or Billy saw you taking the pictures," Frank suggested.

"It's likely they did," Joe responded. "I was standing on third base when I took the photo."

Frank caught his brother's gaze. With a small, almost imperceptible nod to Heather, he said, "Well, let's think on it overnight. It's almost five—quitting time."

Joe nodded. "Let's go." He recognized Frank's unspoken language. Frank wasn't ready to give up for the day, but he wanted privacy to continue talking about the case.

But an hour later, Joe was just as confused as ever. Sitting in their father's study, they'd hashed over every possible connection between Big Ben, Oscar, Billy, Mr. Murphy, and the embezzlement.

"I still don't get where Billy fits in," said Joe. "I mean, is he in with Big Ben? Why would he risk it all by stealing money from the company his grandfather works for? Billy doesn't need the money."

"Don't forget, they were arguing," Frank reminded his brother. "Maybe Big Ben has some kind of hold on Billy." He frowned. "But we still don't even know who Big Ben and his fellow weasel, Oscar, are."

A determined look came over Joe. "But I'm sure going to find out."

*　　*　　*

Frank stared at the video display terminal on the desk in his room, ignoring the morning light that filtered through the window. The disk he'd copied from the stadium's computer was nestled in the disk drive of Frank's computer.

He had set the alarm for six and had been hard at work for over two hours, despite the headache the carbon monoxide had given him, which still lingered from the day before. It was Wednesday, and he and Joe had just three full days, including today, to wrap the case up before their father returned.

Frank was tempted to call his father and explain what had happened on the case so far. But he knew his father well enough to realize that once he heard about the "accidents" with the baseballs and the van, the older Hardy wouldn't want them to go any further with the case until he returned on Saturday. But Frank wasn't one to start an investigation and then let it drop.

Frank pressed a few keys, and the computer screen filled with figures. Frank smiled. Bingo! He had found what he was looking for. He punched up the print command and ran off the results. Then he made an extra copy of the disk, slid both the copy and the printout into his jacket pocket, and headed downstairs.

Joe was in the kitchen, peeling a banana.

"You're up," Frank said as he opened the refrigerator and pulled out the orange juice.

"Your pounding on those computer keys was so loud that you could have awakened the spirit of Christmas past," Joe quipped. He took a bite of the banana and asked, "Find anything?"

"Funny you should ask," Frank replied. "But I'd rather explain it to Mr. Murphy and you at the same time."

"You sure you trust Mr. Murphy enough to tell him what you've found?" Joe asked, finishing off the banana.

"What choice do we have? It's either that or wait until Dad returns."

"No way," Joe said, standing. "I'll never be able to live it down if we back off a simple embezzling case."

"Simple? You've got to be kidding. In the past two days someone tried to kill me with carbon monoxide and steal some photos that could incriminate Mr. Murphy's own grandson. Not to mention that you got nailed with a couple of high-speed baseballs, not so accidentally. And let's not forget those two thugs who paid Dad and us those friendly visits." He turned and headed for the front door. "Come on, let's go."

Once at the stadium, the Hardys found the manager sitting behind his desk, reading the morning paper and drinking a cup of coffee.

"Good morning, guys," Mr. Murphy said over his paper as Frank and Joe entered the office. "I'm glad to see you're okay after that accident yesterday, Frank. Do you think it's related to what's been going on here?"

"Probably," Frank said. Without missing a beat, he added, "We've got something you ought to look at." He took the computer print-out from his jacket pocket and smoothed it open on the desk.

"You see," Frank began, pointing at the computer paper, "someone has programmed the computer ticket program to miss every fortieth ticket sold. The computer hid those sales, in a sense, transferring the assets to another account, one marked 'Miscellaneous' in the computer. The embezzler simply withdrew the money from the miscellaneous account and pocketed it."

Frank glanced up at Mr. Murphy. The manager looked stunned. His mouth was open, and a small blue vein on his right temple pulsed. "How did you find that? I searched those files."

"Part luck, part experience," Frank explained. "The miscellaneous file was buried in the accounting program. I had to figure out the password to find it. The program your accounting department uses is one you can buy in any good computer store. I just ran up the basic language program until I found an anomaly containing the password."

"What was the password?" Mr. Murphy asked.

"Honus Wagner," Frank told him. He crossed his arms over his chest. "This couldn't be done with cash—only with credit-card orders. The computer never registered the transaction and therefore never noticed that the money was missing."

"Who else knew that you had the Honus Wagner card?" Joe asked Mr. Murphy.

"Just about every collector in the nation," Murphy replied. "There are only about fifty Wagner cards left. It's like owning a Van Gogh painting. I get offers all the time."

"We need to narrow it down more than that, Mr. Murphy," Frank said. "What Joe meant is, who in the employment of the Blues organization knew that you had the Wagner card—someone who also has access to the computers."

"Several people," Murphy answered. "The owner, Mr. Barry, is a big collector himself. Some of the secretaries, Heather Hammons, and a few of the maintenance people also knew."

"And Billy," Frank added pointedly.

Murphy shot him a defensive glance. "Of course."

"Where is Billy now?" Joe asked.

"Down in the training room. He was scheduled to replace some fittings in the whirlpool." Murphy's face reddened. "What are you two driving at?"

Frank explained their theory about Joe's accident with the pitching machine to Mr. Murphy. "We now believe Billy did it deliberately," he concluded. "Joe also saw Billy arguing with Ben Norman in one of the VIP boxes yesterday."

Murphy was visibly agitated. His face turned red, and he began fidgeting with the newspaper. "How do you know Big Ben?" he asked.

"We had a run-in with him on Sunday, the day the card arrived at our house," Joe said. "Who is he, anyway?"

Frank looked expectantly at the older man, but Murphy didn't answer Joe's question. Obviously there was something he was keeping from them.

"Who knew that you were sending the Wagner card to our father as a retainer?" asked Frank.

"No one," Murphy replied through clenched teeth.

"Not even Billy?" Frank pressed.

"Billy's not involved in this," Murphy all but shouted.

Frank let out a sigh of frustration. "Look, Mr. Murphy, you hired us to find out who was stealing from the Blues organization. We don't have concrete answers, but we've got some interesting questions. I never really knew Billy in school, but he's tops in computer class and calculus. Billy has the talent to break into a copyrighted program and rewrite the ticket scam into it.''

''But he doesn't have a motive,'' Murphy sputtered.

''Not one that we know about, anyway. But I think it's time we asked him about that.'' Joe rose and headed for the door. ''I'm going to find Billy and bring him up here.''

''We'll wait here,'' Frank said as Joe left the office and headed for the elevator.

The training room and the locker rooms for both the home team and the visitors were on the basement level of the stadium. When Joe stepped from the elevator, he looked around the curved hallway and spotted weight machines through an open doorway.

''Billy,'' he called out, stepping into the room. No answer.

Joe looked around the bright white training room but saw no one there. He looked past the metal body-building machines, running and rowing machines, and a high table for massages.

''Billy,'' he repeated.

Again no answer.

At the far end of the room was a half-opened door, and through it Joe heard the loud sound of water gushing. That must be the whirlpool, he thought. Walking over, he pushed the door fully open, then stepped into the room and looked around.

Two large stainless steel whirlpools took up most of the space. One of the whirlpools was empty, and wrenches and metal fittings cluttered the floor around it. Joe frowned when he saw the other one. Hot water was spilling over the sides and rushing toward and down a floor drain.

Joe shook his head. Billy must have taken a break and forgotten to shut off the water. Walking to the overflowing whirlpool, Joe bent over to shut off the jet valves, taking care not to jostle his left arm in its sling. His hand closed around the hot water valve, and he began turning it clockwise.

Suddenly Joe felt something hard hit him in the back of the head. A searing flash of pain shot through him, and blackness began to crowd out his vision. He let out a yell as he fell headfirst into the hot, swirling water!

Joe blinked, determined to keep from blacking out. He reached for the edge of the whirlpool and tried to raise himself but couldn't. Then a strong hand gripped the back of his neck, forcing his head to remain beneath the water. He held his breath and struggled to raise himself with his good arm, but the blow to the back of his head had stunned him to the point of near unconsciousness, and his collarbone was beginning to throb. He was too weak to fight. It was a struggle just to keep his eyes open!

Then the water began to change colors. First

to a slight pink, then a darker pink, then the colors faded as Joe lost his ability to keep his eyes open.

It was blood, Joe realized. His blood!

He tried one more time to fight against the steel grip around his neck.

Then Joe went limp, and an inky blackness enveloped him.

Chapter

8

THROUGH THE POUNDING in his head Joe was aware of a blinding white light. It was the whitest, brightest light he had ever seen.

And in the center, a pale face surrounded by coppery hair came into focus.

"Are you okay?" the face asked.

"Fine," Joe replied weakly. He took a deep breath, then gagged and coughed up hot water. Joe rolled over on his side, coughing up more.

Then he remembered. Reality set in like concrete. He had been hit in the back of the head and left to drown in the whirlpool. He was soaked, and now that he was out of the hot water, he was beginning to get cold.

"Are you sure you're okay?" Heather repeated.

"Yeah," Joe told her. "I drank a tub of water, but I'll live." Joe turned slightly and looked at her. "How did you find me?" he asked through chattering teeth.

Heather helped Joe to sit up and readjust his sling. Joe grimaced in pain.

"I was walking by the training room and heard the tub overflowing," she told him. "So I came in here and found you bobbing for bubbles."

Joe tried to laugh but managed only a weak, wet cough at her bad pun.

"I called for help as soon as I realized you were still breathing," Heather continued.

"You didn't see anybody else?"

"No," Heather replied, shaking her head.

"Joe!" Frank shouted as he ran into the room.

Joe pressed his good hand to the back of his head. "A few decibels lower," he pleaded.

Frank knelt down next to Joe. "What happened?"

"Someone decided I needed to take a bath—fully clothed," Joe said. A pounding headache was beginning to press itself out from inside his skull.

"I ran down the stairs as soon as Heather called," Frank said. "Mr. Murphy took the elevator."

"Joe!" Mr. Murphy shouted as he joined the group.

Joe grimaced as Frank helped him to his feet.

He took the towel Frank handed him and applied it to the base of his skull, then looked at it. The towel was stained pink, but the bleeding had apparently stopped.

All of a sudden he realized he was shivering from the cold air in the room. "Any dry clothes around here?" he asked Mr. Murphy.

"Might be a stray uniform around someplace," Murphy replied.

Heather headed for the training room. "I'll see what I can find," she offered.

Turning to face Mr. Murphy, Joe said slowly, "I think that you'd better find Billy and have a good, long talk with him."

"You don't think Billy did this, do you?" Mr. Murphy looked shocked.

"I don't know who attacked me," Joe said, trying to be diplomatic. "But Billy was supposed to be here. Maybe he saw someone else do it. Or maybe he did it himself."

"You're in no shape to talk to anyone right now, Joe," Frank cut in. "As soon as Heather finds some clothes for you, I think we ought to get you home and patch you up."

Joe stared at the flowered wallpaper on the kitchen wall and tried not to think about the stinging sensation from the alcohol Frank was daubing on his wound.

"One thing I'll give you credit for," Frank

was saying, "you sure know how to take your lumps."

"Very funny."

"How are your shoulder and collarbone?"

Joe pressed his right hand gingerly to his injured left shoulder. "Okay, I think. I must have landed on my right side before Heather dragged me out of the whirlpool."

"Just like new," Frank announced as he pressed a gauze patch over the wound.

"Swell," said Joe dejectedly. "I feel like a spare tire that's been patched one too many times." He got up slowly, steadying himself on the kitchen table, then headed for the stairs. "I'm going to rest for a minute."

Frank followed. "When you're ready we can go to work to find out who planted the bogus Honus Wagner computer file and transferred ticket money to his own private account."

"But don't you think Billy did it?" Joe asked, confused.

"Billy's not the only one with access to the accounting program, and it doesn't take a *real* genius to break into a program's basic code and do a little rearranging," Frank explained.

"You're giving me a headache just talking about it," he said.

As he closed his bedroom door behind him, Joe heard his brother say, "Even you could do it."

"I heard that!" Joe shouted back, and then he wished he hadn't yelled as a thunderous wave of pain crashed through his head. He lay on his bed and drifted off to sleep almost immediately.

An hour later Joe awoke to the sound of the doorbell. He turned over on his right side, groaning as the tinny tune of "Jingle Bells" chimed through the house. He was trying to think of some way to "accidentally" destroy the thing when the bedroom door opened.

"Hey, buddy," Frank said, appearing in the doorway. "We've got a visitor."

"Tell Chet I've died and the funeral was yesterday," Joe growled.

"It's Heather."

Joe had to keep himself from jumping out of bed. "On my way," he said with a smile.

When Joe entered the den a few minutes later, Frank and Heather were sitting cross-legged on the carpet in front of the fireplace. The roaring fire cast a yellow glow into the room.

When she saw Joe, Heather said, "Good, you're here. How are you feeling?"

"Never been better," Joe said with a laugh. "What's happening?"

"I was just telling Frank that Portside had the potential to become one of the greatest left-handers in baseball history until his accident. Then he was on the verge of being one of the greatest managers when the Oklahoma City club canned him. Call me sentimental, but I want to see the old man get a break.

"Portside told you that he had sent the card to your father as a retainer, didn't he?" Heather asked.

"Yes," Joe replied. "So?"

"Billy was furious that his grandfather sent the Wagner card to your father. Why did Portside do that?"

"Dad refused to take a retainer until he was certain he could take on the case," Joe explained. "I guess Murphy was just anxious to make sure Dad took him seriously."

Heather nodded, then asked, "Where's the card now?"

"Safely hidden," Frank said.

"You don't trust me, Frank?" she teased, one eyebrow raised.

"The fewer people who know the whereabouts of the card, the better," Frank replied firmly. Then he looked closely at Heather. "Why are you asking us all these questions?"

"I was hoping you could fill in the gaps," Heather said. "I'm not a detective, I'm an artist. And I'm worried about Portside."

"Maybe you can help *us* fill in some gaps." Frank turned to Joe and asked, "Did you ever find those concession invoices?"

Joe shook his head. "I checked in every file

I moved yesterday. I was going to look through the rest today.''

"I think I could find them," Heather told them. "Portside put me to work in the filing room one week when Mrs. Shaffer was on vacation. I'm pretty familiar with how the system works."

Joe smiled. "Good. That will save me from another torture session in there."

"I'll get them for you tomorrow and show you where the supplies are stored," she promised.

"First thing tomorrow," Joe said, standing up, "we do a little more checking into Major League Concessions."

Heather checked her watch. "Guess I better get home," she said as she rose. "I'll see you two at the stadium tomorrow."

Frank sighed and shook his head as he watched Joe escort her to the door. Frank could see why Joe was interested in her. Heather was pretty, vivacious, intelligent, and fun to be around.

But Frank was beginning to wonder about her. Did she stop by today to inquire about Joe, or was she pumping them for information? Images appeared in Frank's mind: She had just happened to be passing by the training room right after Joe had gotten knocked out in the whirlpool. And hadn't she been the one to call Joe's name right before he'd been hit with the baseballs from the pitching machine? Had it really been to warn him—or had it been her intention to distract Joe so he wouldn't have time to dodge the balls?

Frank couldn't be sure, but he knew one thing: He was going to keep an eye on Heather from now on.

"Oh, boy," Joe said sarcastically to Frank as they headed out the front door the next morning. "A regular heat wave. The thermometer actually says the temperature has risen to thirty-eight degrees." Joe tapped the outdoor thermometer to make sure it hadn't frozen, then followed his brother to the van, hopping into the passenger seat as Frank turned over the ignition.

Fifteen minutes later they arrived at the stadium. They walked onto the ground floor of the stadium, and Joe's face lit up as he spotted Heather waiting by the elevator.

"Think of anything after I left?" she asked them.

"Well, I'm wondering if there's any leftover inventory from last season?" Frank asked, getting down to business.

"Yeah. A ton of it. Mr. Murphy had ordered it when he thought the Blues would make the play-offs," Heather explained. "As you know, the Blues didn't make it that far. Mr. Barry blew his stack when he heard about all the extra hot dogs we had lying around. Portside tried to sell the stuff to other clubs, but they had their own excess to get rid of.''

''Hmmm. And how about the files on the concession inventory? Can you get those for us now?''

''Sure. Meet me at the freezer locker, down in the basement. That's where the stuff is stored. I'll bring the files down.'' With that Heather turned and entered the elevator.

Frank stared after her. Something still didn't feel right about her sudden eagerness to help them with the case. She seemed a bit *too* eager.

''You coming?'' Joe asked, breaking into Frank's thoughts.

''Yeah,'' said Frank.

When they got to the basement hallway, Frank began to sense that they were not alone. Joe's shout confirmed his suspicion.

''Hey, there's Billy!'' Joe yelled.

As Frank looked up he saw Billy just outside the entrance to the training room, a huge orange pipe wrench in his hand.

In a single quick motion, Billy flung the wrench.

Frank started to run toward his brother, intent on pushing Joe out of the way before he got nailed with the deadly tool. But Frank feared that the wrench would win the race!

Chapter

9

"JOE, WATCH OUT!" Frank shouted and then shoved his brother to the side, against the wall. The pipe wrench hit the wall right where Joe's head had been a second before. The hollow metallic sound echoed throughout the hallway.

"Hey, there he goes!" Joe heard Frank yell. He looked over in time to see Billy dart down the hallway toward the locker room, Frank in hot pursuit.

As Joe took off after them, trying not to disturb his collarbone with the motion, Billy slammed through the doors that led into the visitors' locker room and disappeared.

Joe caught up to Frank just inside the doorway and looked quickly around. Lockers lined three walls of the room, while the fourth wall was empty except for the door that led up to the visitors' dugout. But that door was chained shut. Billy was nowhere to be seen.

"He didn't go out the door," Joe said, pointing out the chain.

"He's got to be here somewhere," Frank said.

Then an idea occurred to Joe. He gestured toward the lockers, which were two feet wide and six feet tall—definitely large enough to hold someone Billy's size. Frank nodded.

One by one, they began throwing lockers open, but Billy wasn't in any of them.

"Where is he?" Joe shouted, slamming his right fist against a locker in frustration.

"Hey!" Frank shouted, pointing above Joe's head.

When Joe looked up, he spotted Billy on top of the lockers. But before he could make a move, Billy jumped down onto Frank, aiming his knees for Frank's chest. Frank was sprawled on the ground and could do nothing when Billy slugged Joe's left shoulder.

Joe yelled out in pain as the fire seared his collarbone. He watched powerlessly as Billy darted to the door and disappeared into the hallway.

Frank pulled himself to his feet and said to Joe, "You okay?"

"Just get him!" Joe yelled. "I'll be fine."

Frank raced into the hallway, but by the time he got there, Billy was no longer in sight.

"Hey, Billy!"

Frank recognized Heather's voice yelling out from the stairwell, and he ran toward her. But when he reached her, he found her sprawled on the steps, several files scattered in disarray around her.

"Are you all right?" Frank asked breathlessly.

Heather nodded.

Frank bounded past her and sprinted up the stairs to the ground floor. He looked both ways through the concession area.

But Billy had disappeared.

"I can't believe we lost him," Frank gasped, still breathing hard from the exertion. He paused a minute to catch his breath and then started back down the stairs.

"Here, let me help you," he offered Heather. She was sitting on one of the steps, collecting the files.

"You two having fun?"

Frank and Heather turned to see Joe walking toward them, grimacing as he rubbed his left arm in its sling.

"How's your shoulder?" Frank asked.

"It's fine," Joe said, but he didn't sound convincing.

"What happened?" Heather asked.

Joe quickly told her. "We didn't even get to talk to him," he finished.

"And now Billy Boy's gotten away—again." Frank turned to Heather. "Well, now that you're down here, we might as well see what you have to show us in the freezer."

Frank helped Heather gather up the last of her files, and then the brothers followed her down the hallway. She stopped in front of an old, thick wooden door.

"This thing must be ancient," Joe commented, rapping on the heavy wood.

"Portside told me it's been here as long as the stadium has," Heather said. "And I believe him." She opened the door, and Joe was struck by a blast of freezing air.

"At least we're dressed for the occasion," Joe observed as he zipped up his parka. He looked at the piles of cardboard cartons lining one wall of the freezer. "What's in all these boxes?" he asked.

"Let's find out," said Frank. "Maybe we can match some of these bills." He took an invoice out of a file and scanned it until he found the invoice number. Then he checked the unopened cartons, stopping by one that had the matching invoice number stamped on it. Beneath the number was another stamp, which read "24 cases hot dogs."

He opened the box and began counting, his breath coming out in white puffs.

"What are you doing?" Heather inquired.

Frank didn't look up. "Checking to see if the stadium received what was ordered. Here." He handed Joe and Heather two other invoices. "Why don't you two check these?"

For ten minutes they counted, checking their numbers against the invoices.

"You guys get what I got?" Frank asked.

"The orders are short," Joe announced.

"Yep."

Heather had a perplexed look on her face. "I don't understand."

"If you check the invoices against what's marked on the outside of the cartons, they match," Frank began. "But if you open the boxes and count what's inside, you come up short on actual inventory."

"A mistake at the warehouse?" Heather asked.

Frank shook his head. "I don't think so. Every middleman has his own middleman. Snyder gets the hot dogs from a processing plant, but before he ships them out to the various teams' concession stands, I think he pulls two or three packages from each box, reboxes them, and sells them."

"He shorts the customer and can even build new inventory from the packages he lifted. That way, he can increase his profit. Not exactly legal, though," Joe concluded.

"You got it, bro," Frank said. He exhaled, expelling a long white cloud into the icy freezer. "This could be completely separate from the computer embezzlement through ticket sales, of course. But at least we're finally getting somewhere. We'd better tell Murphy."

Heather touched Frank's arm to restrain him. "Portside is going to be pretty upset, you know. He thinks of Rocky Snyder as his good friend. They've known each other since their rookie days."

Joe looked at her and raised a brow. "As they say, with friends like that, who needs enemies?"

"Come on," Frank urged. "Let's go."

Just as he turned to leave, however, the large wooden door suddenly slammed shut!

"No!" Frank shouted. He ran to the door and pushed the latch, but the door wouldn't budge. Feeling a sinking sensation in the pit of his stomach, he grabbed the handle and shook the door violently, but he wasn't surprised when it remained closed. Then he heard a faint click, like the sound of a padlock being closed.

Frank turned to Joe and Heather, who both stood speechless, with stunned looks on their faces.

"Someone's got it locked on the other side!" Frank shouted.

Joe darted over to him. "Can we break it down?"

"This thing might as well be solid steel," Frank replied. "It's at least three inches thick and sealed tight to keep in the cold."

The cold! The thought hit Frank like an arctic blast. He glanced at the temperature gauge by the door, but it was frosted over. Using his jacket sleeve, he rubbed away the frost until he could see the glaring white dial and black numbers: *zero degrees!*

Frank scanned the room. It was all enclosed, the door being the only way in or out.

"If we don't break out of here fast," Joe said, voicing Frank's own fear, "this place could be our final, frozen resting place!"

Chapter

10

"GOT ANY IDEAS?" Frank asked Joe and Heather.

Already the cold was pressing against Joe like a steel wall. His toes and fingers and the tip of his nose began to feel numb. He recognized the symptoms as the first signs of frostbite. They had to get out soon or they would freeze to death!

"Let's try kicking it," Joe suggested.

"O-okay," Frank stammered. Joe could see that Frank, too, was feeling the cold, and Heather was jumping up and down to keep from shivering too much.

He and Frank took turns kicking at the latch, hoping they could break the lock on the other side of the latch itself. They tried for several minutes, but the freezing temperature was sapping their strength.

A fan suddenly switched on, circulating the icy air around the freezer. Joe paused to see what the temperature was and saw that it had risen two degrees.

"Our moving about has warmed up the freezer," he told the others. "It's kicked on the fan."

"I-I'm freezing," Heather stuttered, her teeth clicking together.

"We'll get out of here somehow," Joe assured her. "Just remain calm."

"I hope so." Heather's lips were turning blue, and her eyelashes and brows were crusting over with frost.

Frank looked frantically around the room, as if an opening might magically appear. But all he saw were the same four walls.

Hey, wait a minute, he thought. The freezer *was* old. It had probably been put in when the stadium was built.

Frank leaned against the wall next to the door and felt it give. He turned. The wall had been sprayed with a quick-drying, hardened foam used as insulation years ago. He remembered reading that a lot of businesses had used the foam in hopes of saving money but had learned that the insulating factor of the foam decreased over the years, and the walls even began to crumble as they deteriorated.

The foam on the walls of the stadium freezer must be at least twenty-five years old. That's old, Frank thought—old enough to be weak.

Frank stepped back from the wall and kicked out. A second later the look of determination gave way to surprise as his foot smashed into the dried-out foam insulation, sinking five inches into the wall. It stopped only when it hit the plywood outer shell.

Frank let out a loud hoot. "Want to help?" he asked Joe as he continued to kick in the wall.

"You bet!" Joe replied. He, too, began kicking, being careful to hold his left shoulder still. In a few minutes they had cleared a hole in the insulation large enough to crawl through.

All that remained was the outer plywood shell. Taking a deep breath, Frank lashed out with a side kick. The plywood cracked but did not break. Two more kicks, however, and the plywood shattered.

He and Joe quickly helped Heather through to the hallway, then followed.

"Let's get upstairs to a warm office," Joe said, heading for the stairs.

"You bet," agreed Frank. "There's someone we have to talk to."

Still shivering, they took the elevator to the third floor, then rushed down the hallway to Murphy's office. He was just hanging up the phone when they burst in on him.

"What's going on?" Murphy asked, startled.

Frank didn't answer at first. He grabbed the coffeepot, poured a cup of coffee, then handed it to Heather, whose teeth were still chattering.

"Here, this'll warm you up," he said as she gratefully took the mug in her trembling hands.

Joe stomped over to Mr. Murphy's desk. "Your grandson just tried to kill us," he shouted. "Again!"

"What do you mean, Billy tried to kill you?" Murphy sputtered, his face turning red.

Joe took a deep breath, trying to control his anger. "We were checking out the inventory in the freezer when the door suddenly slammed shut and was locked from the outside," he quickly explained. "And just a few minutes before that, Billy threw a wrench at me!"

"I don't believe it," Murphy retorted. "Billy's not that kind of kid."

Frank faced Murphy squarely. Somehow he had to make Murphy be more objective. "Would he steal from you?" Frank asked.

"You've got a lot of nerve." Murphy was practically shouting. "You're off this case, both you and your hotheaded brother."

Frank wasn't about to let him get rid of them that easily. "Look, Mr. Murphy. We were doing this to help you out, but now it's gotten dangerous." His anger helped to relieve the cold that still numbed him. "You tell your grandson to come talk to us. If he doesn't, Joe and I will come looking for him."

"Don't you threaten him!" Murphy shouted.

"Just give him the message," Frank said calmly. He backed away from the desk. "Let's move it, Joe."

Joe headed for the door but then stopped and turned when he realized that Heather wasn't following. "You coming?" he asked her.

Heather remained silent, her brown eyes staring into the coffee she held with both hands in front of her. She looked at Joe and said softly, "I can't. I still believe in him." Then she returned her gaze to the coffee.

Frank grabbed Joe's right arm and pulled him through the door. "That's that, then," Frank said. "Let's go."

Joe followed his brother down the hall. What was going on with Heather, anyway? Joe wondered. The evidence against Billy was overwhelming. It was obvious that Murphy was being overly defensive and unreasonable about Billy. Why was Heather backing him up?

"Hey, shake a leg," Frank said, breaking into Joe's thoughts. He was waiting by the elevator, impatiently tapping his foot and punching the button.

Joe arrived just as the elevator did. He entered

the small compartment in silence and didn't say anything as they rode to the ground floor. Frank finally broke the silence.

"I know you like her, Joe," he said, "but for now, we've got to concentrate on finding Billy and closing this case."

Joe nodded. He knew his brother was right.

"First, I want to check something out at the police station," Frank said as they headed for the van. "Con Riley should still be on duty."

Officer Con Riley was an old friend of the Hardy family and knew the Hardy brothers' record for putting all sorts of criminals behind bars. When Frank followed his brother into the Bayport police station's squad room, Con was the first person he saw. The officer was at his desk, typing.

"Happy holidays," Con said to the Hardys as they walked up to his desk. His smile quickly faded as he read the hard looks on the brothers' faces. He cocked one eyebrow. "Okay, what do you want?"

"I need to ID a character who goes by the name of Big Ben," Frank said, getting right to the point.

"His real name is Ben Norman," Joe added. "I'm not positive, but I would guess he has something to do with gambling on sporting events."

Con leaned back in his chair. "First, you tell

me what you're working on, and then I'll tell you if I can help you. This may be the season for giving, but you know that if Chief Collig finds out about this, I'll be pounding a beat on Christmas Eve." Chief Collig wasn't as supportive of the Hardys' efforts as Con was.

Frank quickly explained about the Honus Wagner card, Stuart and Billy Murphy, and the ticket and concession scam. "I don't know if there's a connection between the tickets and the concession rip-offs. That's one of the reasons we need this info. We need more to go on."

"You sure you're not making all of this up?" Con asked, glancing at his desk calendar. "April Fool's Day is four months away."

"Do we look like we're laughing?" Frank said.

Con gave them an apologetic glance. "Sorry for my little joke."

"Emphasis on *little*," Joe put in, smiling.

"Okay, guys," Con began, leaning forward to type some commands on his computer keyboard. "Let's see what the magic box has to say about Mr. Big Ben. Occupation, bookie. Specialty, sporting events."

"Pro sports," said Frank.

"Pro sports," Con repeated, typing in the correction.

Minutes later, the screen jumped to life, filling

with a computer-generated picture. Below the picture was a long caption.

Frank bent closer and read the screen. Ben Norman, AKA Big Ben; present residence, Oklahoma City, Oklahoma.

"This means there might be a connection between Big Ben and Murphy's stint in Oklahoma," Frank said.

The rest of the report listed various crimes of which Big Ben had been accused. Not the least of them were bookmaking and extortion.

"Thanks, Con," Frank said once he'd finished reading.

"You want a hard copy?" Con offered. "No charge."

"No, but thanks anyway for your help," Frank said.

"Give my regards to your folks," Con replied.

"Sure thing," Frank said. "Lets go home and get some lunch," he said to Joe. They needed something to take away the chill that had settled in their bones, and Aunt Gertrude's stew sat in the fridge just waiting to be heated up and served.

Frank was the first to enter the Hardy home, and he headed immediately for the kitchen and the stew. He had just taken it out of the fridge and put it on the stove when Joe called out to him.

"You'd better come in here, Frank."

"What is it?" Frank asked, heading for the den. But he stopped short when he got there. Joe's back was to Frank.

"What the—" Frank's voice trailed off.

Billy Murphy stood across the room, a .38 revolver aimed at Joe, its hammer locked back and ready to fire!

Chapter

11

"DON'T DO ANYTHING CRAZY, Billy," Frank cautioned in a stern voice.

"He was in the den when I walked in," Joe said over his shoulder.

"I don't want to hurt you," Billy said, his gun hand shaking. "Either of you."

"Then put the gun down," Frank said, keeping his voice calm. It appeared to Frank that Billy was more nervous about the gun than Joe was.

"First give me the card, then I'll just leave," Billy said, his voice quavering.

"What card?" Joe asked.

Billy let out a nervous laugh. "Don't play stupid with me. You know what card. The Honus

Wagner card. The one my grandfather sent to your old man.''

"What do you want with it?" Frank asked.

"I'm going to give it back to my grandfather," Billy replied. "It belongs to him."

"How do we know you'll give it to him?" Frank asked. "From everything we've learned, you're trying to ruin your grandfather."

Billy's face flushed, and he said, "I am *not!*"

Frank couldn't tell if Billy was acting out of rage or guilt. But he did think he knew Billy well enough to doubt that he could be serious about shooting Joe.

"We don't have the card here," Frank explained. "Our dad put it in his safety deposit box before he left town." Frank saw that Billy looked less sure of himself.

"I don't believe you," Billy said, but he sounded doubtful.

"That's your problem," Frank replied steadily. He thought it was time to call Billy's bluff. "We don't have the card, and waving that empty gun isn't going to get it for you."

Billy opened his mouth in surprise. Then, letting out a long sigh, he lowered the hammer.

"I didn't think I could fool you two," he told Frank and Joe. "But I had to try."

Joe stormed over to Billy, his fist clenched, and stood nose to nose with the other boy. "Why'd you try to kill us?" he demanded.

"First me at the whirlpool, and then all of us at the freezer?" Joe's blue eyes bore into Billy.

"I didn't do it, man," Billy replied, flustered.

Frank stepped up behind his brother. "Why did you run when Joe and I called out to you earlier today?"

"Hey, I may not have lived in Bayport very long, but I know you two guys have mean reputations," Billy sputtered.

"What about the whirlpool?" Joe asked quickly. "And rigging the van's exhaust?"

"I don't know anything about it," Billy fired back.

"And the pitching machine?" Joe blurted.

"It w-was an accident."

"The pitching machine can only be loaded manually. We checked it out." Joe gave Billy one more chance to tell the truth.

But Billy wouldn't back down. "That model can be manual or automatic, for your information. I took the automatic arm off after it fired those baseballs at you because *that* was the problem."

Frank had been watching them volley back and forth. It was obvious that neither one of them would back down. Frank didn't completely believe Billy, but he had to admit he put up a convincing front.

"I think a truce is in order," he said, pushing between his brother and Billy.

"Look, Hardy," Billy said, gesturing to Joe, "all I want is the card. It belongs to my grandfather. He's had it since he was a kid."

"No dice," Joe said. "You'll have to talk to my father when he gets back on Saturday."

Billy glared at him in silence, then walked out of the den. Joe followed him to the front door. Once outside, Billy turned and said, "One more thing, Hardy."

"What?"

"Stay away from Heather."

Now it was Joe's turn to glare. "Is that a warning?" he asked.

"It's a threat," Billy retorted. Then he turned and walked away.

Joe slammed the door shut, fuming. Then he said to Frank, "Do you think Heather is getting friendly with me just to find out what I know about Billy and the embezzlement scheme? Is she caught up in the scam?"

"I've wondered about Heather for a while now," Frank said. "But I can't answer your question. One thing I do know is that Major League Concessions works out of Brooklyn. I'd say a little road trip is in order."

"Let's do it." Joe grabbed his jacket and was out the door in a second. Frank grabbed the keys and his jacket and caught up with him.

* * *

The trip to Brooklyn took over an hour. Turning off the highway, Frank steered the van to a residential area known as Park Slope, where Major League Concessions was located. Tucked into the neighborhood was a small area with a few warehouses. Finally Frank spotted the building they were looking for. It was large and old. Its bricks were darkened from age and pollution, and the windows were frosted over by the freezing weather.

Frank parked the van next to the loading dock. Then he hopped into the back of the van.

"What are you doing?" Joe asked from outside the van.

"Getting the pocket copier." Frank rummaged around in a bag of equipment. A moment later he pulled out a palm-sized heat-transfer copier he'd gotten for his birthday and hopped out of the van.

"Good idea," said Joe, flipping his collar up against the wind. He took a quick look around the loading dock, which was empty. It wasn't surprising, he thought, considering it wasn't the season for concession-stand business.

He and Frank made their way around the building to the front entrance. Inside, they found themselves in a small office where a thin, middle-aged secretary sat, typing a letter. Through an open door behind her desk, Joe could see a wide hallway, which probably led to the storage area. Another door had Rocky Snyder's name painted on it in black letters.

The woman stopped typing only to push her black-rimmed glasses back up on the bridge of her nose. "May I help you, gentlemen?" she asked without looking up. The words came out in a nasal Brooklyn accent.

"I'm Max," Frank explained. "This is Herbert. We'd like to see Mr. Snyder."

"He's away on business." The secretary continued typing.

"Shoot," Frank said. "We were supposed to pick up an order for the Bayport Blues."

"A little early to start the season, isn't it?" For the first time she took a second to eye both Frank and Joe. "I suppose you have an order form."

"Yes." Frank patted his pockets. "Have you got the form, Herb?"

Joe followed Frank's lead and patted his pockets. "No. I thought you had it."

"I told you to get it when we were leaving," Frank argued back.

"Hey! I had other things on my mind, Max, okay?" Joe returned.

"Settle down, boys," the woman said, watching them over the tops of her glasses. Then she pushed the frames back up again.

"Could you check with shipping?" Joe asked, sauntering forward and winking at the woman.

He glanced at the nameplate on the desk, which read "Gladys Smith." "Please, Gladys. If we return without the stuff, Mr. Barry will have our hides for his Christmas pudding."

Gladys was blushing from the wink Joe had given her. "Well, I guess I can do that," she said slowly. "You gentlemen wait right here." She stood and started down the hallway.

"Whoa," Frank smirked. "Got an admirer there, Joe."

"Knock it off," said Joe, but he was chuckling, too.

Frank walked over to the office with Rocky Snyder's name marked on it. In a whisper he said to Joe, "Keep a lookout for your new friend." Then he entered the office and shut the door behind him.

He had to move quickly. He didn't have much time, and it didn't help that he really didn't know what he was looking for.

Anything, Frank thought. A file, an invoice—anything.

He opened the top desk drawers and quickly searched around inside them, but he didn't find anything. Closing them, he opened another drawer. Again, nothing.

"I'm sorry, but we don't have a record of your order," Frank heard Gladys say.

Frank froze. Why hadn't Joe signaled?

"Oh." Joe's voice sounded startled. Obviously the secretary had taken him by surprise.

"Where's your friend?" Gladys asked.

"He, uh, went to the bathroom," Joe said.

"What's wrong?" Gladys's voice was rising, as if she was excited or worried.

"I feel faint," Frank heard Joe say.

Frank shook his head. What was Joe up to?

"Maybe it's the flu," came Joe's voice again, followed by a low groan.

"Oh, dear," Gladys exclaimed. "Can I do anything to help?"

"I just need to sit down for a minute," Joe said.

"Here," Gladys said. "Follow me. We have a nice lounge room. Let me walk you back there."

"Thank you," Joe said weakly.

Then there was silence.

Frank quickly went back to work. He opened two more drawers but found nothing unusual. With a sigh of frustration, he pulled open the bottom file drawer on the right side and flipped through the files. Halfway through, he saw one that was labeled "Portside." He pulled it out and opened it.

Inside were small slips of paper the size of grocery receipts. Scribbled on the paper were the names of sports teams, and Frank noticed some major league baseball teams. Next to the team names were numbers.

Point spreads, Frank thought with growing excitement. He didn't see any of Murphy's past or present teams listed, but Portside had definitely been gambling on other major league teams.

Next to the point spreads were betting odds and dollar figures. One slip of paper added up to over three thousand dollars. He could hardly believe his eyes.

Frank listened for sounds of Gladys returning. Hearing nothing, he pulled the copier from his pocket and flipped it on. He placed the head of the copier on the top slip and scanned down the small piece of paper. Heat-transfer copy paper began snaking out of one end of the copier. It took him only a few seconds, but it seemed like forever. Joe and Gladys would be back any second. He copied three more slips, wishing the copier was faster. Beads of sweat popped up on his forehead.

Finally he was done. Turning off the copier, he put it and the copies in his jacket pocket. Then he closed the file, shoved it back into its proper place, shut the drawer, and tiptoed to the door.

He opened it slightly and peeked out. The room was empty. Joe must have found a way to keep Gladys in the back room. Slipping from the office, he started down the hallway.

He found the lounge next to the warehouse. Joe and Gladys were both sitting in metal chairs.

Joe hopped up when he caught sight of Frank. "Thanks, Gladys," he said with a smile. "I feel much better now."

"My pleasure," said Gladys. "Happy holidays."

Rather than head back to the front entrance, Frank and Joe walked casually through the warehouse toward the loading dock and the van.

"Find anything?" Joe whispered.

"Yup. Betting slips," Frank said. "Looks like Murphy *did* bet on baseball games, but—"

Frank stopped short when a familiar, threatening voice bellowed out in the warehouse.

"Well, if it isn't Tweedledum and his brother, Tweedledumber."

Whirling around, Frank saw that Big Ben was standing behind them, his arms crossed, a sick smile on his face.

Frank and Joe took off at the same instant, sprinting for the door that led to the loading platform. They were halfway across the warehouse's concrete floor when the barking began. Glancing behind him, Frank saw two large amber-colored pit bulls bounding toward them, their mouths pulled back to reveal pointed yellow teeth.

Frank and Joe were twenty yards from the door when Frank suddenly felt his foot catch on something. He flew forward and slammed onto the concrete floor.

Joe stopped and spun around to see Frank lying next to the wooden pallet he'd tripped on. Joe's mouth dropped open in horror.

The pit bulls were on Frank like wolves on fresh meat. One dog's jaw clamped viciously around Frank's right wrist while the second got ready to sink his teeth into Frank's throat!

Chapter

12

LOOKING UP, Frank saw one of the pit bulls bare his teeth just inches from his throat. The dog's bloodshot eyes chilled Frank to the bone. Frank rolled away from the dog and onto his stomach.

He gasped as one of the pit bulls snapped at his arm. He braced himself for the pain, but luckily the dog only got a hold on his jacket with his sharp teeth. Frank's adrenaline was pumping from fear, but he couldn't move.

"Rex! Samson! Heel!" It was Big Ben who shouted the command. Low, guttural growls told Frank the dogs weren't happy their master had called them off.

The pit bull that had Frank by the sleeve

remained still but did not loosen his bite on Frank's jacket.

"Call him off," Joe ordered. If he had been close enough, Joe could have placekicked one dog across the warehouse, and then Frank could have handled the other pit bull.

"Sure thing," Big Ben agreed, flashing his sick smile. "Got 'em covered, Oscar?"

"Like a glove," Oscar replied.

Joe had been so preoccupied with the attack dogs that he hadn't seen Big Ben's companion. Oscar had appeared next to Big Ben, and he held a Colt .45 automatic in his right hand.

"Rex! Samson!" Big Ben called out. "Home!"

Frank got to his feet when the dog let go of his jacket. Simultaneously both dogs bounded over to Big Ben, circled behind him, and then sat at the big man's heels. Big Ben pulled two dog biscuits from his pocket and tossed them to the pit bulls, who caught them in midair and swallowed them in one gulp.

"You boys could take a lesson from these dogs," Big Ben called to Frank and Joe. "Do as you're told, and you get rewarded. Isn't that right, Oscar?"

"That's right, Big Ben," Oscar replied. His thin face was twitching, and his bushy brows were set in a scowl.

"If you had only given us the Wagner card at the shopping mall, you two wouldn't be in such trouble now," Big Ben said condescendingly. "As it is, you've gotten yourselves involved in a situation that's way over your heads, boys."

"We don't have the card. What do you and your dogs plan on doing about it?" Frank was usually calm, but Joe could tell he'd reached the boiling point.

"I like gentlemen who are direct and to the point." Big Ben moved closer to the Hardys, followed by Oscar and the two pit bulls. "The meat of the matter is this: I want the card, and I want it now. Not tomorrow. Today."

"The card is in a safety deposit box in Bayport," Frank said.

"Yes, so I've been told," Big Ben replied with a sigh.

Frank and Joe glanced at each other. Both were thinking the same thing. They both knew that the Honus Wagner card was in the floor safe in Fenton Hardy's office. Frank had told Billy that the card was in a safety deposit box to keep him from searching the house. Frank hadn't told the lie to anyone else, and neither had Joe.

That meant Billy was working with Big Ben to steal the card from his grandfather—and probably to embezzle funds from the Blues as well.

"Why do you want the card so badly?" Frank asked Big Ben.

"What are we going to do now?" Big Ben

sighed dramatically. "Play twenty questions? This is not a game. This is reality."

Big Ben lurched forward and made a swing at Joe, but Joe managed to jump out of the way.

"Okay," Joe said through clenched teeth. "Here's some reality for you."

He cocked back his fist and fired a right cross that connected with Big Ben's lower jawbone.

Big Ben staggered back, tripping over Rex, Samson, and Oscar, all four sprawling onto the floor.

"Let's hit the road!" Frank shouted, and he sprinted for the van.

Joe was at Frank's heels.

The dogs growled as they took off after the brothers at Big Ben's command, but Frank and Joe were a step ahead of them.

Joe looked behind him at the dogs, which were coming on fast. He got a glimpse of Big Ben rolling himself off Oscar. Joe couldn't see the .45, but he knew it wouldn't take Big Ben long to find it.

Bursting through the door to the loading dock, Frank and Joe jumped down from the platform and raced to the van. Frank ran to the driver's side, and when Joe hopped into the passenger's seat, his brother was firing the van's engine to life. A split second later, the pit bulls were barking and growling outside the van, trying to get at Joe and Frank.

Frank stomped on the accelerator, and the van pitched forward and away from the dock, its rear fishtailing as the tires spun on the icy asphalt. Frank slowed the van enough to maneuver a turn onto the street.

As he got back onto the highway, Frank turned to his brother and asked, "Okay, what were Big Ben and Oscar doing at Major League Concessions?"

"You tell me," said Joe. "You're the one with the computer-capacity memory."

Frank took a deep breath. "Here's what we know so far: Stuart Murphy was fired as manager of the Oklahoma City Cavalry expansion team because of his gambling. Now Murphy's job with the Blues is on the line because of embezzlement. Rocky Snyder owns both the Albany Governors and Major League Concessions, which supplies concession items to the Bayport Blues. Hurting the Blues' reputation by getting Murphy fired can only help Snyder. And Big Ben and Oscar seemed right at home at Major League Concessions." Frank paused.

"Now, we know Big Ben is a bookie, and he wants the card, which belongs to Stuart Murphy. Maybe Murphy owes him a large sum. . . . What if Murphy was actually embezzling the money himself?"

"You mean, to pay off money he owes Big Ben?"

Frank nodded. "Right."

"And the connection between Snyder and Big Ben?"

"There's the mystery," Frank replied.

It was dark by the time they returned to Bayport. Frank parked the van in the garage and locked the door.

Once in the house, Joe headed upstairs while Frank turned on the security system.

What troubled Frank was that he didn't know whom to trust.

First there was Stuart "Portside" Murphy and his $100,000 baseball card. Then there was Billy Murphy, a quiet kid who suddenly came on bold enough to threaten Joe. Heather Hammons and her ever-present 35-millimeter camera were mixed up in all of this somehow. And what did a bookmaker from Oklahoma, his sidekick, and the owner of a rival Triple-A club have to do with all of this? And who had planted the bogus ticket program in the Blues' computer?

Everything seemed to start with the Honus Wagner card. A simple, two-by-three-inch, seventy-year-old piece of cardboard. Frank decided to take a look at the card, which he hadn't seen since Sunday. He got it out of the safe and sat down on a lounge chair, studying the tinted picture of the ballplayer in the funny pants. The card was in pretty good shape for being seventy years old—no creases or tears in the cardboard. And to think a ten-year-old had played with it, not realizing— Suddenly an amazing idea occurred to Frank.

"Hey, Joe!" he called. When his brother appeared, Frank told Joe he wanted to follow a hunch.

"McKay knows more about the card than anybody," Frank said. "I think we should have a talk with him." He glanced at his watch. "Six o'clock. The mall's open until nine. Let's go!"

Joe kept pace with Frank as they walked up the stairs to the second floor of stores at the Bayport Mall. Frank took a right and headed straight to the Old Ball Park.

As soon as he stepped into the shop, Frank felt uneasy. Mr. McKay wasn't in his usual spot behind the counter, and the place was empty of customers.

"Mr. McKay," Frank called out. He leaned over the counter and strained to see into the back storeroom.

"Maybe he went to get a soda or something," Joe suggested.

Frank frowned. "He wouldn't leave his store unattended."

Frank went around the counter and pushed through the curtains that led to the back room. He stopped short, letting out a gasp.

Sprawled out on the floor was a body. It was Lyle McKay, and the back of his head was covered with blood. Cards, uniforms, pennants—all kinds of baseball memorabilia lay strewn around the narrow space.

Frank knelt down and checked McKay's pulse, then turned and looked at Joe.

"He's dead!"

Chapter

13

"ARE YOU SURE?" Joe asked, coming up next to Frank.

Frank nodded. "You'd better call the police."

An hour later McKay's body had been taken to the coroner's office, and Con Riley had finished writing Joe and Frank's statement into his logbook.

"From the looks of things," Officer Riley said, gesturing toward the articles that littered the storeroom floor, "I'd say the old man put up quite a struggle."

Frank nodded, but Joe noticed an impatient look on his face. "Yeah," Frank said, shifting his gaze out into the mall and the gawking crowd. "Can we go now?"

"I guess," Officer Riley said. He gave them a stern look. "But you two know the rules."

"Yeah," Joe piped up. "Don't leave town."

Frank and Joe pushed their way through the crowd, ignoring the questions and stares of the onlookers, and made their way to an exit. Joe checked his watch as they stepped out into the dark, cold winter night. It was only eight o'clock, but all the events of the day made it feel as though it were much later.

The darkness had dropped the temperature to below freezing, and Joe felt his face and ears numbing in the crisp air. As they neared the van, he heard Frank mumble, "The police have it wrong, but they'll figure it out soon enough."

"What are you talking about?" asked Joe.

"Mr. McKay didn't fight with anybody before he was killed."

"How do you know?"

"Well," Frank began slowly, "if the articles from the shelves had been thrown down during the struggle, some of the items would have blood splatters on them. But I checked while you called the police." Frank paused.

"And?" Joe prompted.

"And there isn't any blood on the baseball cards, the hats, or any of the stuff. The blood is under the items, on the floor."

"Meaning that Mr. McKay was killed first and then the killer tore up the shelves, vandalizing the place, or maybe looking for something," Joe finished for him.

Frank nodded. "Not just any old something. The killer wanted the Honus Wagner card."

Joe stopped dead in his tracks. "That's supposed to be back in Dad's safe."

"Supposed to be," Frank said. "I took this out of the safe when we got home," he added, sliding the card out of his pocket. "I was tricked by that old man."

"Are you sure?"

"Remember when we took the card to Mr. McKay to have him authenticate it?" Frank asked.

"Yeah."

"He showed us a reprint. A really good reprint that had been printed to look exactly like the seventy-year-old baseball card. A likeness so real that Mr. McKay was able to switch the cards before my eyes, and I didn't catch it. See this coloring?" Frank went on. "It's duller than the other card. That's why I thought it was older, but apparently I was wrong."

Joe was stunned. He blurted out, "He's had the original the whole time, and—"

"The reprint's been safely tucked away in Dad's safe," Frank finished. "McKay told us he had wanted one all his life, remember? And he finally got it. Pulled the old sleight-of-hand right in front of our eyes."

"And look at what it cost him," Joe said, shaking his head.

They reached the van and hopped in.

"Someone had to have found out that the cards had been switched," said Frank. "But who?"

"Pick a suspect," Joe declared. "Big Ben, Oscar, Billy. They've all tried to get the card from us."

"And don't forget Rocky Snyder," Frank added. "Yet we still don't know how the card fits into the embezzlement."

Joe sighed. "So now what's the plan?"

"There's no way of knowing if the killer found the real Honus Wagner card or not," Frank said. "I think a nocturnal visit to Mr. McKay's home is in order. Let's get the phone book and check for his address."

Frank hopped in the back of the van and flipped on one of the back overhead lights. Pulling a battered Bayport telephone book from one of the cabinets, he opened it and flipped through it.

"Got it," he announced a moment later.

"Where?" Joe called from his seat.

"Shady Valley Mobile Home Park." Frank climbed back into the driver's seat, started the van, and headed for the mall exit.

Shady Valley Mobile Home Park, located in

the northwest corner of Bayport, was only about a ten-minute drive from the mall.

Joe shook his head as they entered the park. "I've never understood why they call this Shady Valley," he said. "There isn't a tree in sight."

Frank looked out his window at the barren, flat expanse of land. Trailers were lined up in rows, and a small lane snaked up and down between them.

Spotting a row of mailboxes lined up in front of a building by the entrance to the trailer park, Frank stopped the van and hopped out. He scanned the mailboxes until he found one with Lyle McKay's name on it.

"Lot 52," Frank said as he hopped back into the van. He shifted the transmission into drive and pulled off, winding slowly up and down the rows until he saw the marker for lot 52.

"Do you see what I see?" Frank asked Joe as he slowly drove the van past the long, low mobile home.

"Porch light's on," Joe said. "And there's a light on in a front room."

"Any movement inside?"

Joe shook his head. "Not that I can see."

Frank sped up the van. "We'll circle back and park the van near the entrance."

Once Frank had pulled to a stop, Joe went into the back, rummaged through Frank's bag, and pulled out two police flashlights. They were each fifteen inches long and heavy. If he and Frank ran into trouble, the flashlights could double as billy clubs.

"Just in case we run into any creeps," he told Frank, handing him a flashlight.

Joe's shoulder and collarbone were pulsing with a dull pain as they walked toward the lot. He didn't know if it was because of the cold air or the heightened anticipation of running into McKay's killer. He and Frank moved quietly, avoiding the front road and heading down the alley between the row where McKay's home was and the row of homes behind it.

As they approached lot 52, Frank noticed with relief that the rear of the mobile home was dark. Before trying to get in, Frank and Joe crouched and ran to the front of the mobile home. They both sneaked looks into two lit windows, but no one seemed to be inside.

"Hold my flashlight," Frank whispered once they had reached the back door.

Frank handed his flashlight to Joe and pulled out a pocketknife. He flipped opened the blade and crept up the three steps to the door. He was about to start jimmying open the lock when he felt it give under the slight pressure of his hand.

"It's open," Frank whispered to Joe, taking his flashlight from his brother. "Looks like there's already been a visitor here."

"Or *is* a visitor," cautioned Joe.

"Ready?"

Joe nodded.

Frank pushed the door open slowly and stepped in. Joe followed behind him. It only took a moment for their eyes to adjust to the darkness, and Frank saw that they had stepped into a hallway made narrow by the boxes that lined one side of the wall from floor to ceiling. Enough light from the front room reached the hallway so that they could read the sides of the boxes. Each was marked with the same label—"Cards"—written with a felt-tip marker in a thin scrawl.

A door was to Frank's right. He glanced down at the crack between the floor and the door. Seeing that the light was off, he opened the door slowly, stuck the flashlight in, and flicked it on. The room was washed in the bright white of the powerful beam. As with the hallway, the room was filled with boxes labeled "Cards."

McKay was apparently a serious collector, Frank thought. He and Joe would have to check out the room once they had made sure the coast was clear. Flicking off his flashlight so as not to attract any attention, he stepped back and shut the door.

Joe was pointing down the hallway toward the front of the mobile home. In answer to Joe's unspoken question, Frank nodded, and they walked slowly to the end of the hallway, then stopped to listen.

Frank peered through the doorway, which opened into the kitchen and then the living room. Both rooms were lit up, but there wasn't anyone in them. Staying away from the windows, Frank quickly went through to the hallway on the other side of the living room. It led to a front bedroom, which was also empty, illuminated only by its ceiling light.

"Someone's definitely been here," Joe whispered to him as he returned to the living room. Joe pointed to the fake mantel that had been ripped from above the fireplace, leaving hunks of plaster on the floor.

Frank glanced around the room, which was sparsely furnished with an easy chair, a couch, and a table with a lamp, all neatly arranged. The walls of the kitchen and living room held photos of famous baseball players, many of them signed.

"That's funny," he said. "It doesn't look like they did much serious searching. That fireplace looks to be the only thing that's been disturbed."

"Let's hope McKay put the card someplace simple," said Joe.

Frank nodded. "And that the killer didn't already find it." He walked over to the couch. "This is as good a place as any to start."

"I'm going to check the bedroom," Joe said, heading for the small hallway off the living room.

As with the living room, the bedroom was furnished simply—a bed, a night table with a lamp, and a dresser. There, too, the walls were covered with photos of baseball players.

Getting down to business, Joe began with the dresser but found nothing. Then he checked the bed, lifting the mattress to look between it and the box springs. Moving to the night table, Joe found a book entitled *The Official Price Guide to Baseball Cards* sitting next to the table lamp. He picked it up and flipped through it. He didn't really expect McKay to have put the card in such an obvious place, but he couldn't overlook anything.

The closet was next. It was small and held McKay's shirts, suits, and shoes. He sure was meticulously neat, Joe thought as he went through the orderly rows. But the closet was a bust, too. Shaking his head, Joe rejoined Frank in the living room. His brother was just replacing the cushion of the easy chair.

"Nothing," Joe said with disgust.

"Well, let's see if we find anything in that room with the cards," Frank suggested.

They had started toward the rear of the mobile home when they heard a car pulling up in front.

"Looks like we've got company," Joe whispered.

He and Frank dashed back through the kitchen to the darkened hallway just as the engine of the car was shut off. Moments later they heard someone trying to turn the doorknob of the mobile home's front door. It must be locked, Joe thought. Then the thudding sounds of someone pushing against the door filled the mobile home.

The door snapped open, and he and Frank ducked further back into the darkness of the hall, remaining just close enough so they could still see into the lit rooms.

Billy Murphy entered the living room, a crowbar in his right hand. He walked to the center of the room, then stopped and looked around.

Seeing that Billy had turned his back to them, Joe signaled to Frank with a nod of his head. Frank nodded in turn, and a split second later, the Hardys sprinted through the kitchen and into the living room.

"Nice of you to drop in," Joe said as he grabbed Billy with his good arm and spun him around.

Billy looked surprised, but not too surprised to swing the crowbar at Joe's head. Joe ducked easily out of the way, then came back and planted a solid right in Billy's stomach. Billy groaned and doubled over. Then Frank, coming to his brother's aid, lashed out with a karate chop to Billy's right wrist, and the crowbar dropped to the carpeted floor.

"You've got some explaining to do," Joe

growled as Frank caught both of Billy's arms and locked them behind his back in an iron grip.

"Take a flying leap, Hardy," Billy spat out.

Frank saw the fire that raged in his brother's eyes as Joe came over and shouted, "Why did you kill McKay? Was that card worth killing a man for?"

Billy refused to be intimidated by Joe. "What are you talking about?"

"Someone killed Lyle McKay at the mall a couple of hours ago and then went searching for a valuable baseball card," Frank said. "What I want to know is how you knew McKay had it."

Billy's mouth dropped open. "Mr. McKay's dead?"

"Yeah," Joe said. "You can stop playing innocent now."

"But—" Billy began.

"Billy didn't kill McKay," said a deep voice behind the Hardys.

Frank let go of Billy, and he and Joe turned at the same time.

Big Ben was standing at the front door, holding a Colt .45 automatic that was pointed right at them.

Chapter

14

"MOVE," Big Ben ordered, waving the .45.

Frank and Joe moved away from Billy.

"And drop those flashlights."

They let the lights fall to the floor.

Frank's gaze raced over the small rooms of the mobile home, trying to find something to distract Big Ben. Keeping his voice as calm as possible, Frank asked, "You killed McKay?"

Big Ben sighed. "My, my, my. Do you really expect me to confess to *you* if I did kill McKay?"

"Humor us," said Joe.

"Why? What good will it do you once you're in your graves?"

"You said no one would get hurt," Billy said in a high-pitched, panicked voice.

"And you said you could deliver the card," Big Ben shot back.

"I can." Billy sounded desperate.

"How did you know McKay had the card?" Frank asked Billy.

"I—" Billy began, but he was cut off by Big Ben.

"Shut up and just get the card."

Billy looked at Frank and Joe. Frank could tell by the nervousness in the young man's eyes that Billy was an unwilling participant in Big Ben's plans.

"First you have to let Frank and Joe go," Billy said.

Big Ben's face flushed red with anger. "You get the card or you'll be the first to drop." He pulled back the pistol's hammer. *"Now!"*

Billy backed away from Big Ben. He walked slowly around the room. Then, after pausing for a moment, he turned and stepped to the wall behind the easy chair. Frank watched closely as Billy took down a framed picture, flipped it over, and pulled a card from the back. Frank was pretty sure that the picture was a photo of Lyle McKay and Mickey Mantle. Another glance confirmed Frank's guess that Billy was holding the Honus Wagner card.

Billy tossed the framed picture onto a chair and looked at the card.

"So that's the Mantle the old man meant!" Big Ben exclaimed.

Frank's mind clicked into action. Now he understood why the back door had been open and why the fake mantel had been ripped from the wall. Big Ben had already made one trip to the mobile home. He must have gotten McKay to tell him where the card was—probably right before he killed the old man.

"This belongs to my grandfather," Billy said softly, bringing Frank's attention back to the trailer.

"Things change, boy," Big Ben said. "Give me that."

Billy looked at Big Ben.

Frank felt a rush of concern when he saw the expression in Billy's eyes. He looked frantic, as if he was about to do something crazy, like rush the big man. Big Ben wouldn't hesitate to kill Billy—Frank had no doubt of it.

"Don't do it, Billy," Frank cautioned. "The card isn't worth more than your life."

Billy jerked his head toward Frank. "It is to me," he said.

"I'm weary of this," Big Ben said. "If he thinks his life is worth the card, so be it."

Big Ben raised the gun and pointed it at Billy.

Suddenly a loud voice ripped into the mobile home from the doorway behind Big Ben.

"SMILE!"

Big Ben whirled around, and at the same time, a brilliant flash lit up the dark night behind the door.

Crying out, Big Ben threw his left arm up to cover his eyes. His right arm swung wildly, and the .45 exploded, blasting a hole in the ceiling.

Joe saw his chance, and he didn't waste an instant. He leapt at Big Ben's back, planting his right shoulder between the man's shoulder blades and pushing both of them through the doorway.

Joe felt the flashes of pain rip through his upper torso as he slammed into the ground on his right side. His left shoulder and collarbone erupted in pain, but he rolled over and pushed himself upright.

Big Ben had already scrambled to his feet, but Joe saw that his right hand was no longer holding the .45. Gritting his teeth against the pain in his shoulder, Joe started for the big man, but the fall had slowed his reflexes. Before he'd taken more than a step or two, Big Ben had jumped into his BMW and was gone.

"Are you okay?"

Joe turned and saw Heather standing outside the door. Her camera and its flash attachment were hanging from her neck.

"Where did you come from?" he asked.

"Let's get out of here," Frank cut in from the doorway. Billy was standing next to him. "Someone's bound to call the cops."

Joe nodded. He and Frank always cooperated with the police, but their report would have to wait until later, when they had learned all the details.

As quickly as they could, the foursome ran between the two rows of mobile homes and hopped into the van. Frank started it up and pulled out.

Joe held his left shoulder, grimacing in pain. He didn't feel any better when he looked back to the bench seat, where Billy and Heather sat, holding hands.

"Now," Joe began. His teeth were clenched, half from pain, half from frustration. He was determined to get the truth from Billy and Heather once and for all. "What were you doing at McKay's?" he asked Heather.

"I saw Big Ben forcing Billy into his BMW at the stadium." She squeezed Billy's hand. "I had to follow."

"Where's your car?" Frank asked, looking at her in the rearview mirror.

"I took a taxi. I didn't want Big Ben to spot my car."

Joe turned a hard look on Billy, but before he could say anything, Billy spoke.

"I know. I've got some explaining to do."

"It can wait until we get you to our house," Frank said.

*   *   *

137

Frank, Joe, Billy, and Heather sat around the table in the Hardy kitchen. Four mugs of steaming cocoa were in front of them, but no one was drinking.

"My grandfather told me what you two were the day he hired you to work at the stadium," Billy was saying. He twisted his mug on the table as he spoke.

"How much does your grandfather owe Big Ben?" Frank asked.

"A hundred thousand bucks."

Joe raised his eyebrows. "That's a familiar figure," he said. "The price of the card."

Billy nodded.

"Is your grandfather guilty?" Joe asked.

When Billy didn't reply, Joe turned to Heather. "How much have you known all along?"

"I didn't want to tell you the truth," Heather said. "I wanted to protect Portside and Billy."

Joe leaned forward. "What truth?" he asked.

Frank had remained silent, listening to Billy and Heather and trying to piece it all together in his mind. Now it was Frank who answered Joe's question.

"That Billy was embezzling the ticket money," Frank said.

Billy seemed startled but then hung his head in his hands. "Right," he said miserably.

"Mr. Murphy found out about the concession scam and was set to blow the whistle on Snyder," Frank went on to explain. "But Snyder had an ace up his sleeve."

Frank reached inside his coat pocket for the copies of betting slips he had made in Snyder's office and tossed them in front of Billy. "These slips could prove that Stuart Murphy was gambling on baseball," Frank said.

"That's a lie!" Billy cried, jerking up straight in his chair.

"Maybe," Frank said, "but you weren't going to take that chance. Your grandfather is known as a heavy gambler on sporting events. Maybe those slips couldn't prove anything, but the scandal would have been enough to end any chances of your grandfather continuing to work in baseball."

"Snyder is a snake," Billy blurted out. "He approached me when we first moved to Bayport last spring and said he would turn the slips over to the minor league commissioner if I didn't put the program into the system. He claimed he had bought the betting slips from Big Ben."

Frank nodded. So *that* was the connection between Big Ben and Snyder.

"Somehow Big Ben and Snyder became partners in the embezzling scheme. But that wasn't enough for Big Ben," Billy went on in a bitter voice. "He wanted to swap the card for what Grandfather owed him."

"And when he found out Portside had sent the

card to our father, he decided to get it back—at any cost," Frank said.

"Big Ben is a fanatical baseball card collector," Billy explained. "I'm the one who told him my grandfather had sent the card to your dad. I thought he would back off once he knew we didn't have it anymore."

"Bad guess," Joe put in.

"Don't I know it," Billy agreed. "He and Oscar followed you to the baseball shop in the mall after I told them where the card was. I really did try to break up the fight that day. Oscar and Ben are the ones who sabotaged your van and tried to kill you. And they made me come over here and threaten you. I was too afraid of them not to do what they said."

"How did Big Ben know that McKay had the Wagner card?" Joe asked. "He thought *we* had it."

Billy shrugged. "McKay was offering it to the highest bidder."

"And because he had stolen it," Frank added, "he couldn't put it on the open market."

Frank glanced at his watch. It was nearly midnight. "It's late. Tomorrow we all go to the police and clear this up," he said, getting up from the table.

"You two better spend the night here," Joe said. "Heather can have Aunt Gertrude's room. Billy, I hope you don't mind the couch."

"I should call my grandfather and tell him where I am," Billy said. He picked up the phone and started dialing.

Frank paused at the foot of the stairs. "One more thing," he asked Billy. "How did you know where McKay had hidden the real Wagner card?"

Billy placed the phone back in its cradle.

"I was leaving the stadium when Big Ben pulled up and forced me into the car. He told me he was tired of waiting to buy the card, had approached McKay, and had muscled him until McKay told him that it was behind the Mantle. Big Ben didn't say anything about killing McKay, I swear. Anyway, Ben and Oscar tore down the fake mantel and didn't find anything. That's when Ben came to me. He thought I might know where it was. It was just a lucky guess on my part."

"I think you'd better let me hold on to the card," Frank said, holding out his hand.

Billy hesitated, then took the baseball card out of his shirt pocket and handed it to Frank.

Frank took the card and started upstairs.

"Hello, Grandfather," he heard Billy say as he closed his bedroom door.

The foursome were up and dressed by seven the next morning. By eight they had eaten and were on their way to the police station in the van.

Frank felt easier than he had all week. The real Honus Wagner card rested securely in the inside pocket of his jacket, and he had no doubt that Big Ben, Oscar, and Snyder would be in custody soon after the police were informed of their crimes.

They were several blocks from the police station when the van's cellular phone chirped.

Joe picked up the handset with his right hand and said hello.

Frank saw a worried look come over his brother's face. A second later Joe hit the speaker button, and a scared voice spoke.

"J-Joe?"

It was Callie, Frank realized, and she sounded terrified!

There was a scuffling noise over the phone line, and a squeal from Callie.

"That you, Hardy?"

Frank recognized Big Ben's deep bass voice.

"What's going on, you creep?" Joe growled into the speaker.

"I'll put this as simply as possible. Bring the card to the stadium in ten minutes, or I kill Callie Shaw!"

Chapter

15

FRANK COULDN'T BELIEVE his ears. Big Ben was holding Callie hostage! He made a fast right at the next intersection and headed toward the stadium, driving as fast as was safely possible.

When they arrived at the stadium, Frank hopped from the van and ran inside to the ground floor. Joe, Billy, and Heather were right behind him.

"That's far enough," Big Ben's voice boomed.

Frank and the others slid to a halt. At the far end of the hall, near the elevators, stood Big Ben and Oscar. Oscar gripped Callie tightly with his left arm and pressed the muzzle of a .38 revolver into her side with his other hand.

Rocky Snyder was on Big Ben's right, and he held another pistol.

"All I want is the card," Big Ben said. "Then you kids can all go home and play."

"Let Callie go," Frank ordered.

"Do you think I'm a fool?" Big Ben scoffed.

"I'd do what he says," Rocky said, waving his pistol.

Frank thought fast. "Are you willing to take a murder rap along with your two friends?" he called to Rocky.

"Huh?" Rocky seemed genuinely confused. He didn't know about McKay's murder, Frank realized. That could work in their favor.

"Seven seconds," Big Ben said, ignoring Rocky.

"Your partner murdered Lyle McKay last night," Joe told Snyder. "And your helping him now makes you an accomplice."

"Is that true?" Rocky asked Big Ben. "Did you kill McKay?"

Big Ben didn't answer. "Time's up. The card, please." He held out his right hand.

Frank and the others remained still.

Rocky moved closer to the big man. "I said, is it true?"

"It is of no consequence to you, *partner*," Big Ben said.

Rocky started to raise his pistol and point it at Big Ben, but Big Ben swiftly grabbed Rocky's arm and twisted it so that the gun pointed away from him and at the foursome.

The gun went off, causing Frank, Joe, Billy, and Heather to scramble.

Frank heard the bullet hit the concrete wall just over his head. Without pausing, he started for Oscar and Callie. He hoped the fight between Big Ben and Rocky would distract Oscar, but the short goon just pressed the gun deeper into Callie's side.

"Not a smart move," Oscar said in his high-pitched voice.

"Frank," Callie said at the same time, desperation in her voice.

Frank froze, motioning to the others to do the same. They all watched helplessly as Big Ben slammed a large right fist into Rocky's face and Rocky hit the floor, unconscious. Then Big Ben picked up the gun and turned to the group.

"The card, *now!*"

They all turned in surprise as the elevator bell rang. The door whooshed open, and Mr. Murphy stepped out.

"What—?" He stopped short when he saw the guns.

"Just a little trade," Big Ben said. "The Honus Wagner card for the lives of these kids."

Frank glanced at the scared faces that were looking at him expectantly. With a sigh, he reached inside his jacket.

"Easy," Oscar warned, pressing the gun harder into Callie's side.

Slowly Frank pulled the card from his outside jacket pocket and held it up.

"Walk it over here . . . *slowly*," Big Ben ordered.

Frank approached the big man.

"That's close enough," Big Ben said when Frank was an arm's length away.

Frank held the card up. But just as Big Ben reached out to take it, Frank ripped the baseball card in half.

Big Ben's eyes widened, and he gasped.

Frank ripped it into quarters.

"You—you—you're mad!" Big Ben shouted. "That's worth a hundred thousand dollars!"

Grinning, Frank ripped it into eighths and tossed the pieces at Big Ben's feet.

"No!" Billy yelled from behind Frank. Frank heard footsteps, then felt himself being spun around. He saw the rage in Billy's eyes a second before Billy's fist swung toward him.

Throwing up his left arm, Frank stopped the oncoming punch and knocked Billy back. Then, still aware of Big Ben standing behind him, he whirled back around.

Big Ben was now on his knees, picking up the pieces of the destroyed card.

"It's gone, it's gone," Big Ben wailed. "It's gone!" He looked up suddenly, then got to his feet with amazing speed. "And so are you," he growled at Frank, raising the gun.

Instinctively, Frank shot out at Big Ben with a spinning karate kick, his left heel hitting squarely across the left side of Big Ben's face. A deep moan sputtered from the man, and Big Ben hit the concrete. He was out cold.

Joe sprinted toward Oscar, and at the same time, Callie slammed her right elbow into Oscar's sternum and broke free of his grasp. Oscar groaned and stepped back, but he managed to hold on to his gun. Lifting his arm unsteadily toward Joe, he fired the .38.

Joe heard the bullet whiz past him, then heard Heather's scream behind him.

"No!"

Joe turned just long enough to see that Billy was lying on the ground, with Heather kneeling beside him. But Oscar was running down the wide corridor now, and Joe didn't have time to stop. He bolted after him.

Oscar was fast, and Joe was slowed by the sling holding his left arm. He grabbed the sling and lifted it off, throwing it to the ground. He grimaced as he let his left arm fall to his side, the pain from the bruised collarbone sending needle-sharp pangs through his left shoulder.

Oscar turned to his right and ran out of the building and into the stadium's seats.

Joe turned onto a closer ramp. He nearly slipped on a patch of ice, but he caught himself.

A second later he sprinted into the brilliant light of the early-morning winter sun.

A shot rang out, and a chunk of concrete exploded by Joe's head. Keeping low, Joe ran to a row of seats and ducked behind them. When he peeked out, he saw that Oscar was one section over to the left, and that the other man was starting down the stadium steps toward the field. Joe sprang up and ran down the steps of his section, running parallel to Oscar.

Oscar reached the bottom and hopped the chain-link fence. This time Joe was ready when Oscar turned and fired. Joe squatted down but didn't slow his pace until he had reached the fence. Taking a deep breath, he hopped over the fence and onto the field. He stiffened when Oscar fired, but once again he missed.

That's three, Joe thought. Three more and he's out of ammo.

Joe gritted his teeth in pain, but he forced himself to sprint forward. He almost tripped when his feet struck an object, kicking it in front of him. Glancing down, Joe spotted a battered old baseball. Without slowing down, he scooped it up with his right hand as he went past.

Oscar turned and aimed the .38 again, but Joe zigzagged out of the way as he shot. Suddenly he stumbled to his knees. He hadn't been ready for the sudden incline of the pitcher's mound.

Oscar was just past second base and heading into center field. In another minute he'd be gone!

It's now or never, Joe thought. He fired the baseball at the fleeing man with all the force he could muster.

Oscar turned and raised the gun to shoot again but didn't have time to fire. The baseball slammed into his left temple, and as he fell back, the gun fired harmlessly into the air.

Joe scrambled to his feet, ran to the prone man, and snatched up the gun. The smaller man was only semiconscious, Joe saw, and a bruise was quickly swelling on the left side of his head.

Joe lifted the man to his feet and pushed him toward the stands. Oscar stumbled forward, wobbling as he walked.

Mr. Murphy came down from the stands and met Joe at the chain-link fence. "Say, that was some fastball," he said. "I saw it from the ramp." He unlocked a small gate to let Joe and Oscar through. "You ever consider professional baseball as a career?"

"It couldn't be more fun than what I'm doing now," Joe said with a smile.

Mr. Murphy grabbed Oscar by the arm and escorted him up the stands and back inside.

Joe quickly saw that everything was under control inside. Big Ben was still unconscious. Frank was standing over Rocky Snyder, who had regained consciousness and was sitting against the wall. Callie stood near Frank.

"Are you okay?" Frank asked Joe.

Joe smiled back. "Nothing a short rest won't fix. Against the wall," he ordered Oscar, gesturing with the gun to a spot next to Snyder.

"I called the police," Heather said, coming over to the Hardys. Billy was next to her, pressing a towel against the side of his head.

"You okay?" Joe asked.

"Yeah," Billy said. "The bullet just grazed me. I've got a terrible headache, though."

"It'll go away in a few hours," Joe assured him. He turned to Rocky and Oscar. "What I'd like to know is which one of you tried to drown me in the whirlpool?"

"Wasn't me," Rocky said quickly. "I don't mind cheating on hot dog orders, but murder's out of my league."

Joe fired a stone-cold look at Oscar.

"Big Ben ordered me to do it," Oscar admitted, staring at the floor.

"The reason I threw that wrench right before you were locked in the freezer," Billy explained, "was to try to scare you away. I'd overheard what Big Ben had planned for you."

"I'm sorry, Frank," said Callie. "I came down here to talk to you, and the fat man grabbed me."

"I'm just glad you're okay," Frank told her.

Billy looked at Frank. "I appreciate what you and your brother have done for Grandfather and me," he said. His face was pale, and the look in his eyes was sad. "But you shouldn't have destroyed the card." He held his free hand out and showed Frank the torn pieces of the Wagner card resting in his palm.

Frank smiled.

"I don't think it's very funny," Billy blurted out angrily.

Frank reached inside his jacket. "That's the reprint," he said, indicating the torn pieces Billy held in his trembling hand. He pulled out the 1911 Honus Wagner card and held it out for Billy. "Here's the real card."

Billy's face went blank. Then, throwing the torn pieces up in the air, he grabbed the real Honus Wagner eagerly from Frank, a huge grin on his face. "Thank you, Frank! I can't believe it! The real thing!"

"Well, what's going on here?" A voice rang out from the ground floor entrance.

Frank looked behind Heather and Billy as Fenton Hardy strolled up to the group.

"Dad!" Joe exclaimed. "We weren't expecting you back until tomorrow."

"I just drove in about ten minutes ago. I cleared my other case a day early," Fenton explained, "so I thought I'd get started on Mr. Murphy's problem." His eyes took in the scene. "But I guess I arrived a little late."

"Your boys did a fine job," Mr. Murphy told Fenton, beaming.

"Yeah. I can tell," Fenton replied, looking at Big Ben, Oscar, and Rocky.

Mr. Murphy cleared his throat. "But I'm afraid I have a little confession to make."

"Let me guess," Frank interrupted. "You didn't send the card to Dad as a retainer, but just to keep it safe."

"Yes," Mr. Murphy said with surprise. "How did you know?"

"With someone like Big Ben around, it wasn't hard to figure out," Frank replied.

Billy walked up to his grandfather and handed him the Honus Wagner card.

"Keep it," Mr. Murphy said, grasping Billy around his shoulders. "It's time to pass it on. It's my Christmas gift to you." The older man smiled, his eyes filling up with tears.

"Thanks, Portside," Billy said, his voice cracking with emotion.

"Speaking of Christmas gifts . . ." Joe said to Frank, nodding at Callie.

Frank swallowed. Callie was staring at him, her brown eyes twinkling expectantly. "Frank Hardy!" she said, stomping her right foot. "You don't mean to say you haven't found a gift for me yet?''

Frank quickly started out the stadium's exit, pulling his brother along with him. ''Come on, Joe, this is going to be tougher than any case. Let's go shopping!''

Frank and Joe's next case:

Frank's old friend Ray Adamec, former ace navy pilot, has been hired to test pilot a superhot, supersleek jet—the MAX 1. But then Ray disappears, and the MAX 1 is nowhere to be found. Frank's pilot license proves invaluable as the Hardys take control of the MAX 2. Their mission: find Ray and recover the MAX 1 before it falls into dangerous hands.

Finding a clue to the whereabouts of the MAX 1 in the Utah desert, the boys set out to investigate. Instead they find themselves outnumbered and outgunned in a high-tech, high-altitude air battle. They've flown into the middle of a subversive plot posing a deadly threat to the top levels of the U.S. space program and the U.S. government . . . in *Flight Into Danger*, Case #47 in The Hardy Boys Casefiles™.